You're the password to my life

HAPPY Birthday

from Vedant

Also by Sudeep Nagarkar

Sorry, You're Not My Type

It Started With a Friend Request

That's the Way We Met

Few Things Left Unsaid

You're the password to my life

Sudeep nagarkar

RANDOM HOUSE INDIA

Published by Random House India in 2014
Third impression in 2015

Random House Publishers India Pvt Ltd
7th Floor, Infinity Tower C, DLF Cyber City
Gurgaon – 122002
Haryana

Random House Group Limited
20 Vauxhall Bridge Road
London SW1V 2SA
United Kingdom

978 81 8400 584 4

Typeset in Adobe Garamond Pro by R. Ajith Kumar

Printed and bound in India by Replika Press Private Limited

A PENGUIN RANDOM HOUSE COMPANY

To the eternal bond that Virat and Kavya share

Zindagi ko badalne me waqt nahi lagta,
Par kabhi kabhi waqt ko badalne me zindagi lag jati hai!!

Contents

Prologue

We all have that one person in our lives in whose absence our existence seems utterly meaningless. For some people, that person is a friend—a family you *choose* instead of being forced into liking. No matter how much you argue with your friends over little things, ultimately you love them for exactly who they are. None of those petty, expensive gifts or sweet words mean anything if one can't appreciate the little things that matter.

Rohan was lucky enough to have the best of both: a friend to live for and a love to die for. A friend who would confidently lie to his parents just to go out with him and a girlfriend who was slowly and discreetly penetrating his heart and soul.

It was the evening of Rohan's relationship anniversary. Rohan had left for his girlfriend Riddhima's place and his friend Virat, too, was on his way. Rohan had made all the preparations for a perfect evening. As he took out his mobile phone from his pocket, he scrolled through Riddhima's pictures in his gallery for a while, then read the text message he had received, and started typing a reply:

You will look ravishing covered in my kisses. You always ask me whether you are better than my ex or not, so let me tell you the truth today—no one can be compared to you, my love. I love you so much and I wonder to myself why? You know what they say—when you know why you like someone, it's a crush and when you can't think of a reason or explanation, it's love.

He read the message once again before pressing the send button. He then thought of deleting the text message from his phone. After all, it had only been a day since they started seeing each other. He feared what Riddhima would think about him. But the best conversations are those that never take place, like the messages that we never send.

Rohan reached Riddhima's house and knocked on the door. She let him inside, though something had changed this time; earlier he used to visit her to learn French while now he was here to teach her how to French kiss, if the stars favoured him. He called Virat to ask him where he was and how long he'd take to reach.

'I am on my way. Will reach in half an hour. Extremely sorry, buddy. I am still stuck in traffic,' Virat lied.

He was not struck in traffic but caught up in another meeting—one with his best friend. A girl can be your best friend, your worst enemy, or your worst night depends upon how you treat her. Virat treated her like a princess but always asked her when would she start looking for a guy to fall in love with to which she would reply, 'I don't need someone so mature that I can't act immaturely around him. What I need is someone who adores my immaturity and maturely understands me.' They'd end up fighting over issues like these and would stop talking to each other for days.

She was supposed to travel back to her hometown that night, all by herself. He never liked the fact that she travelled alone. But she loved adventures and it was beyond Virat's control to win an argument with her.

Virat was about to reach Rohan's place when suddenly he took a U-turn in high speed. The other cars came to a halt the moment Virat took the sudden turn and sped away. While he was waiting for the signal to turn green, he received a message. He immediately called on the unknown number and before the person on the other end could explain the whole thing, he ended the call. Suddenly, he felt numb—like his whole world had come crashing down. He couldn't believe his ears. It was, by far, the worst news of his life.

His hands shivered as he accelerated the car. After a few minutes, he got a call from Rohan again.

'Where are you? Stop following girls and come here right away.'

'Rohan, I'm not coming. I am extremely sorry but I need to see someone urgently. Please don't take this the wrong way,' Virat said with a heavy voice.

'What happened?' Rohan asked sensing the gravity of the situation.

Without uttering a word, Virat disconnected the call and parked his car. He got out and started walking when he realized that he'd forgotten to lock the car, yet again.

'How many times do I need to tell you to check whether the doors have been locked properly or not ? You are so careless, Virat. This is unacceptable.' He remembered her chiding him and a tear rolled down his eyes.

All the crazy moments that they had spent together came rushing back like a flashback in front of his eyes. He remembered their long drives and the way she tickled him sitting beside him in the car. An empty smile, unspoken words, and a broken heart; it was killing him. Their relationship did not flourish as intended. Perhaps, it would go somewhere better. All the good memories and the precious moments they had shared with each other had been scattered in a fraction of a second.

Sometimes we play with our lives, but when the time comes for us to get serious, life plays with us. Rohan was expecting Virat to celebrate his newfound happiness with him, but now even Rohan was worried for Virat. Riddhima was confused by the way Rohan was acting and wanted to know what had happened.

Whenever he faced a difficult time, she would be the first person to be by his side. Now he was missing that support of hers. Virat was missing the support of his best friend, Kavya.

A Slightly Insane Friendship

Mid July, 2009

'Kavya, what are you doing here at this hour? You act like my mom. She also had this habit of waking me up early in the morning for no reason whatsoever. It's so annoying!' Virat muttered still half-asleep. Kavya was kicking his butt in an attempt to wake him up.

Virat and Kavya were both students at Biosis College, Pune.

I wanna make up right now, na na…wish we never broke up right now, na na…

The song was playing on repeat on the stereo and Virat slept without a care in the world. Kavya kept a duplicate key of his room with her precisely for situations like these.

If it were up to Virat, he would sleep all through the day.

'You can never get up on your own, can you? You

should throw away your alarm clock. It's of no use,' Kavya complained shaking him up.

Kavya was a tomboy, completely extrovert in nature. She made friends easily unlike Virat and loved playing sports and riding a bike. Although slightly plump, she carried herself with grace and was always full of energy. She never wore anything that would make her look like a slut. She was a hardcore foodie at heart and loved to experiment with her taste buds. Her favourite hobby was teasing boys and she didn't spare Virat whenever she got a chance.

Kavya stayed in Kothrud, Pune. She was extremely bold and forthright, and did not care if people took her the wrong way.

'How can you kick me in my own house?' Virat looked annoyingly at Kavya with his eyes half open.

'Oh please! This is not your house. This wouldn't even classify as a "house". Look at that dirty underwear of yours hanging on the rope. It's so old it's covered in holes! And those socks of yours? They stink so bad that I need to carry a room freshener with me every time I come to your house,' Kavya said with an expression of disgust on her face.

He barely made note of her complaints and went back to sleep, asking her not to disturb him for another 15 minutes.

Virat was a smart and witty boy, with an extremely good sense of humour. His only vice was that he was extremely lazy. Kavya would try her best to talk him out of sleeping so late, but he wouldn't listen. He always wore a stubble on his fair skinned face and the style helped him woo girls. Like Kavya, he would never bother himself with what people thought about him and was never ashamed to express what he felt. Though he would take his time to befriend people, he was never outrightly rude to anyone. He feared getting into a serious relationship as the early demise of his parents had scarred him forever. He knew how to charm everyone in his presence and could talk to anyone with ease. He stayed with his aunt in Mumbai during his school days and later, when he started going to Boisis College to study Commerce, he took up a flat on rent near his college.

He met Kavya in the same college and they hit it off instantly. She tolerated him and adored him while he had her back, always. All the other girls? Well, they were friends. Friends with 'benefits'.

'Get up, you kumbhkaran. Look at how late it is. I hope you remember we were supposed to go shopping today,' Kavya said and went into the kitchen to prepare breakfast.

By the time she entered the bedroom, Virat had taken a bath and was getting ready.

'That is so sweet of you. That's why I call you my best friend,' she said pulling his cheeks.

'Stop sugarcoating me. I said I'll come and I always live up to my promise. So let's go,' he said adjusting the collar of his t-shirt.

'Wear your pants, at least,' Kavya said pointing to the towel wrapped around his waist.

'Stop instructing me on the proper dress code when you aren't dressed in salwar kameez either,' he laughed looking at the skirt she was wearing.

'Who do you think you are, a stud?' Kavya asked.

Virat ignored the question and grabbed a comb from the dressing table, eating his breakfast simultaneously. This annoyed Kavya. To set him straight, Kavya knew just what to do. Virat had a few oversized shirts in his wardrobe that he had never worn before.

'What are you doing?' Virat asked her when she picked up one of the oversized shirts and went to the washroom to change.

'You'll see in a minute,' Kavya replied cheekily as she closed the door of the bathroom. What excited Kavya was a nightmare to Virat. When she came out, she was wearing nothing but an XXL size shirt with a waist belt. The shirt barely covered her thighs.

'Have you lost your mind?' he screamed.

'If you can wear those tiny boxers of yours and roam around freely in the house, why can't I go out shopping like this? Doesn't it look sexy?' Kavya asked checking herself out in the mirror.

'I am not coming with you if you are going out wearing that. Tell me, you are kidding, right?' Virat was completely baffled.

'Don't you dare challenge me. If you lose, tonight's drinks are on you.'

Saying so, Kavya pulled Virat by the hand and took him downstairs. She refused to go via his car and ignited her scooty. Virat was completely embarrassed. He looked around to see if anyone was watching them. Kavya was enjoying Virat's embarrassment and couldn't control her laughter. While driving, Kavya's shirt would slide up a bit, and Virat would try and pull it down for her, much to Kavya's amusement. Whenever the scooty would halt due to heavy traffic, they would become the centre of attraction as all eyes would be fixed on them. All Virat could do was hide his face under the helmet.

'Kavya, this is not done. Can't we just go back to our room?' Virat pleaded.

Kavya was in no mood to listen and continued to drive until they reached SGS mall on MG Road. Even the person who handled their parking ticket in the mall took his own time to check out Kavya.

'You son of a bitch…' Virat was unable to control his anger but calmed down when Kavya pinched his thigh.

He had never witnessed such an embarrassing situation before in his entire life and decided not to wear his tiny boxers, not even at home. Theirs was a crazy relationship where nothing was off limits.

'It's not over yet. We still have to go shopping inside the mall,' Kavya winked at Virat.

Virat had no other option than to comply with her wishes. From the security guards to each and every person in SGS mall, everyone stared at them, probably because she looked weird to them or because they wondered why Virat was on the verge of crying even when he was with a sexy-looking girl. Kavya was enjoying herself to the fullest. She was happy that she had won the bet and that Virat would now have to foot the bill. They shopped for her and unsurprisingly, Virat took a keen interest in selecting her outfit so she couldn't humiliate him again.

'Are you enjoying, darling?' Kavya said pulling his cheeks as they stood by the billing counter of Westside.

'I will respond suitably when the odds are in my favour,' he replied as Kavya smiled looking at him.

They left the mall and rushed back to Virat's apartment. This was not the first time that Kavya had messed around with him. She could do so repeatedly because they shared such a strong bond with each other. Isn't this what true friendship is all about? Doing all those crazy things that you can't do with anyone else? Once they entered his flat, Virat and Kavya burst into laughter. They were completely crazy and loved being with each other. Virat and Kavya's connection was above time and space.

'Kavya, tell me something...didn't you feel awkward this morning when you went out in that outfit?' Virat asked.

'I did feel awkward, but that's fine. Paagalpanti is the

trademark of our relationship. Moreover, I could only do so because you were there with me in your boxers,' Kavya winked.

They were both enjoying drinks at the Swig lounge in Koregaon Park. Virat had lost a challenge he had never accepted in the first place. But you can't win an argument with girls, can you? Swig was one of the coolest places in Pune where you could just lose yourself in the crowd. With an amazing ambience in the evening, the place was an attraction to youngsters and the college-going crowd of the city. It had a prominent bar right at the centre, with wooden tables and chairs, and beautiful stained glass lamps that hung above each table, creating an ambiance of warmth. Virat and Kavya loved coming to this place, especially on Tuesdays when most drinks were served at discounted prices during 'Happy Hours'.

'Cheers!' Virat said raising a toast to their friendship. It was his fourth glass of the evening.

'Tell me seriously, who was that girl you were talking to yesterday? I've never seen you with her before,' Kavya said giving him an odd look.

'Are you talking about the girl who was wearing a blue dress?' he asked trying to recall.

'Oh, so you even remember the colour of her dress! You were getting so close with her that I thought...you know...'

'Oh, shut up. I spoke to her for the first time yesterday. I had my reasons. Her name is Mahek. And anyway, I have decided to be serious now. I mean not with her but…you know…I want to be in a committed relationship now. No hanky panky,' Virat stammered.

'Oh really? Is it you talking or the bottle?' Kavya laughed.

'I am serious, Kavya. I was talking to her to confirm whether she would be joining Salsa classes or not.'

'Ok, so then?'

'Then what? She is joining. She is an expert at dance and you know how pathetic I am. So I thought maybe she could teach me?'

Kavya couldn't stop laughing at the thought of Virat and Mehak as dance partners. She didn't know if she was imagining things due to the effect of alcohol or was Virat seriously in love. Virat had never been serious about a relationship before although he had dated many girls in the past. So it was quite strange for Kavya to hear from Virat that he was actually getting serious about love. The only serious relationship he had was with Kavya. But it was pure friendship. She decided to ignore his ramblings till he sobered up. She was a bit high as well and decided to leave the matter be. Generally, friends get serious about something or someone in a drunken state. Virat was no different. She called for the waiter.

'Can I get you anything, ma'am?' the waiter asked politely.

'Ma'am my foot. Tell me, are you giving birth to the chicken? It's been more than an hour since we ordered the dish. Where is it?'

The waiter immediately left to enquire the reason for the delay while Virat kept staring at Kavya after her sudden outburst. The waiter brought out the dish the very next moment and Virat was about to ask for the bill when Kavya shouted again, 'Manager, see the oldie there. Oh god, I think he's dead.'

A middle-aged guy in his mid-30s was sitting adjacent to them and was resting his head on the table after having a drink too much.

Kavya thought of annoying the guy and continued, 'Manager, I am serious. See this old uncle here? He's dead.'

Virat was used to her antics, especially when she was drunk. They laughed as the people sitting around them started looking at them as if they had come from a different planet altogether. After sometime, when the situation was under control and that oldie had left the place, she insisted they leave the lounge without paying the bill. Virat didn't agree in the beginning but then thought of trying it for the thrill. They tried to act casual so that the waiters didn't catch their attention.

'I am going to quietly move out by pretending to be on a call. Once I leave, you can join me in a couple of minutes. You can even come later as they don't really question girls.'

Saying so, Virat moved outside pretending that he was not getting network coverage in the room and slowly walked towards his bike. When he saw no one was noticing him, he sat on the bike and ignited it so that they could run away as soon as Kavya came out. He kept the ignition on just in case they had to make a quick escape. After some time, Kavya came out and casually walked towards the bike as if nothing had happened. As she came closer, she increased her pace.

'Fast…sit…sit…sit…' Virat whispered.

She quickly sat on the bike and they sped away. She turned to see the guard running out of the lounge with the bill in his hand. But Virat raced the bike at bullet speed.

'How did you get out so smoothly?' Virat asked.

'I asked for directions to the washroom and slowly slipped out instead. The manager seemed to doubt me, but I maintained my cool and walked at a casual pace so that the guard standing outside wouldn't stop me.'

They high-fived each other and screamed loudly in joy.

Friendship isn't about who you have known the longest. It's about who came and never left your side even when you committed a crime. In this world where everything seems uncertain, only one thing was definite: Virat and Kavya's friendship…beyond words, beyond time, and beyond distance.

After returning from the lounge, they went to FC road as Virat wanted to eat chocolate paan. Kavya saw a man selling soap bubbles on the road.

'Virat…even I want to blow those soap bubbles,' Kavya

said in a childish manner pointing towards the vendor selling them.

Virat obliged to avoid the similar chaos that had occured a few minutes ago at the lounge. He knew she would create havoc if he didn't buy her those soap bubbles. Little did he know that there was no stopping her and that she would go wilder with each act. As soon as he purchased it, she started blowing bubbles on passersby and troubling them. It became difficult for Virat to control her but even amid this chaos, he couldn't help but laugh at her childishness.

Eventually, Virat took her by the hand and dragged her away from the scene before she could make life miserable for other people. She continued blowing the bubbles sitting behind on the bike. She saw two girls on a scooty parallel to them. The bad girl in her awakened and seconds later, she started bothering them.

'Are you lesbians? You want to try a threesome?' she teased the girls.

'Yeah, please take her along with you. Make her sit between you. She is in a real need of a threesome,' Virat added and started laughing.

Without speaking a word, the girls raced their scooty and ran away. Virat and Kavya had fun eve-teasing all the bikers they crossed, till they reached his apartment.

'What a day it was. I will never forget this my entire life,' Virat sighed as he parked the bike.

'Seriously. We had an awesome time together. We should

do this more often,' Kavya laughed trying to walk properly. The effect of alcohol was taking its toll on her. Virat helped her by holding her hands and taking her upstairs.

'You are staying here tonight. I am not letting you go home in this condition.'

'No, I have to go. Bye,' said Kavya trying to push Virat away.

Virat threatened to inform her parents. He took her inside and made her sit on the couch. She relaxed a bit and started laughing again, without a reason. Virat freshened up and decided to make some Maggi for the two of them. Kavya always loved her Maggi with a seasoning of oregano. She never missed an opportunity to eat it whenever she stayed back at Virat's apartment. While Virat was in the kitchen, Kavya opened his laptop to browse through the folders.

'Virat, where are my Accounts assignment's pictures?' she asked.

'Now why do you need them at this hour? Don't tell me you are going to write it now,' Virat shouted from the kitchen.

'No, I just wanted to see them.'

'They are in the Daily chores folder, E drive.'

Virat poured out the cooked Maggie from the saucepan into a dish and was about to put ketchup on top when he realized that the folder contained some B-grade movies. He kept the ketchup aside and ran into the bedroom to stop Kavya from accessing his folder in time. But it was too late!

'So these are your daily chores?' Kavya teased, turning the laptop towards him.

Virat tried to snatch the laptop away from her but even in her tipsy state she wouldn't let him take it easily, and put up quite a fight.

'Kavya, this is not fair yaar. Some things are really personal and even you should not touch them,' he pleaded.

However, Kavya didn't show him any mercy. She in fact insisted that they watch one of the movies together while eating Maggi. Virat flatly refused but ultimately gave up when he realized that arguing with Kavya would be futile. He made himself comfortable on the bed, next to Kavya, and played a random movie from the folder.

'I don't want to watch this one. Play the other one which had…' Virat stopped her short saying all movies had the same content and it didn't really matter which one they watched.

With every noodle she slurped, she watched the movie with more curiosity. It was the first time she was watching anything like this and was enjoying herself thoroughly.

'See, this guy looks like you,' she said pointing towards the hero of the movie.

'Shut up. Look at the girl; she looks exactly the way you were looking in the morning wearing that sultry dress,' Virat laughed.

Before Kavya could finish her Maggi, Virat fell asleep. She shut down the laptop and smiled thinking about all the fun they had together. Though Kavya behaved like a kid, Virat loved the child in her. She would always say, 'I don't need anyone who is mature enough to stop me from acting immature. What I need is someone who can adore my immaturity and maturely understand me.' No one, except for Virat, would be able to tolerate Kavya's childish behaviour post drinking. Similarly no one could tolerate Virat's untidy nature but Kavya. They were perfectly made for each other; friends who did silly stuff together, laughed at each other when they fell, and lived life their way without giving a damn to the people around them.

More Than 'Just Friends'

'Mahek, I heard you're participating in the dance competition. Is that true?' Virat asked her as they walked around the college campus.

'Yes, I love dancing and want to pursue it as a career option. So I gave my name for the competition,' Mehak answered.

Mehak was the college hottie and Virat had fallen head over heels for her the moment he laid his eyes on her. She was looking ravishing in a white dress that day. Her thick black hair fell loosely on her shoulders. Her dazzling chocolate brown eyes framed by long lashes that she flicked constantly could brighten anyone's world. Her cherry lips looked like a frozen rose, dangerous but beautiful, and her milky white skin could mesmerize anyone. She was the most gorgeous woman he had ever seen, like a painting of a goddess brought to life. When she smiled, the world would sigh with contentment. When she laughed, the world would laugh with her. And if she shed a tear, the whole world would want to comfort her. She wore the same perfume everyday—Elizabeth Arden 5th Avenue—and one could get a whiff of her from a mile away. She was full of confidence which reflected in her cute smile. She was fond of dancing and dreamt of becoming a salsa trainer, and eventually starting an event management company of her own.

Mahek had enrolled in the dance competition that was going to take place between the Junior and Senior Wings of Biosis College. The winner would get a chance to join a professional salsa group, which was really something. Virat had no interest in winning but decided to participate as it was the perfect opportunity to get close to her.

'I am participating as well. I hope we win,' Virat said gazing at her eyes, pretending to sound confident.

'We, what do you mean "we"?' She seemed puzzled.

'Yeah. We are going to be partners, right?' Virat muttered in a soft voice.

'When did I agree to that?' she asked and started to walk ahead.

'Oh, come on. I am not that bad at dancing,' he stated.

'I have seen you dance at the club with Kavya. You are not bad. You are terrible.'

'You can teach me, perhaps…'

For the first time, Virat feared talking to a girl. The more he thought about it, the more he felt like he was in love. Though Virat and Mahek had been going to the same college for over a year, they had never really interacted much with each other. Kavya did talk to her often, and was friends with her, but Virat hardly did. According to him, she was not meant for casual dating, but someone to fall in love with. He had dated many girls in the past but chose to stay away from Mahek and the likes of her. However, the idea of being serious in life made him fall for Mehak eventually. He wondered why he wanted to be in a serious relationship in the first place, but never found the right answer. So he assumed it to be love.

'What's wrong, Mr Stud?' Kavya asked patting him on his back. Mahek had left by then.

'Nothing,' Virat said as he continued walking alone, lost in his thoughts.

'Maybe I can help you. I'm good friends with her,' Kavya added.

The moment he heard Kavya say she was friends with Mahek, he jumped up in joy. His happiness had no limits. He pleaded with Kavya to make a case for him with Mahek so that she saw him favourably.

'What will I get? I deserve something in return,' Kavya winked.

'How rude! You can't do something this pint-sized for your best friend?' Virat pleaded.

'No. If you are willing to give me whatever it is that I ask for in return, I'll do it.'

'And what's that?'

'I need a promise from you. Promise me that once you get into a relationship, nothing will change between us and you won't act like one of those emotionless guys who forget their friends once they find a girlfriend to love. We will still act insane at pubs and run away without paying bills. We will continue teasing bikers late at night, and you will never stop making Maggie for me. Promise me, everything will be the same even after you're committed to her,' Kavya said.

Virat hugged her and assured her that nothing would alter his love for her.

'Don't worry. When I'll ask her out, I will clearly mention that along with a smart, handsome guy, she'll need to deal with a stupid, dumb, and idiotic girl too as a complementary gift.'

Kavya pinched him and smiled. They walked together towards the classroom and sat beside Mehak. There were no lectures as they had to submit their assignments in college the next day. Kavya had already plotted a plan to get Virat and Mehak closer and started to implement it on Mehak. They were chit-chatting when Virat joined them. Mehak gave him the cold shoulder, making Virat feel uneasy. Just then, he received a call from his uncle and went outside to answer it. In the meantime, Mehak and Kavya continued talking, Virat being the topic of discussion. Kavya flaunted his positive attributes to impress Mehak although in reality, Virat couldn't even keep his room tidy. She kept praising him in front of Mehak till Virat returned.

'Let's leave, buddy,' Kavya told Virat as he walked in.

'Where to?' he asked in a surprised tone.

'I am taking Mehak and you out on a date. Up for it?' Kavya teased him.

Virat felt like hitting Kavya with a hammer that very moment.

'Chill, we are going for a movie. I hope you don't mind,' Mehak said in her sweet voice looking at Virat.

'Are you mad? Why would I mind? I am on cloud nine,' Virat added, elated.

'What?' Mehak said giving him a puzzled look.

Kavya nudged him with her elbow and signalled him to come with them. Virat followed both the girls out without uttering a word. There were no lectures all through the day so Kavya had planned for a movie to give them an opportunity to spend some time together. Though they had to submit their assignments the next day, it hardly bothered them. It really doesn't bother students unless they want to impress the professors.

All three of them reached E-Square cinema and booked tickets for the next show of *500 Days of Summer*. Virat was overjoyed since it was his first outing with Mehak. He prayed it would turn into a date in the future. She swept him off his feet whenever their eyes met. For the first time he felt special, like he had been searching for someone special all these years and had finally found her. But he felt a void inside since he didn't know how to act around her.

'Let's go eat something. We still have an hour left,' Virat said looking at his watch.

Mehak agreed and all of them went to the food court.

'Mehak, you've never had a boyfriend?' Kavya asked her on purpose.

'No, I am kinda afraid of relationships,' she said resting her hands on the table.

'Me too. I think we're a perfect match for each other,' joked Virat.

'Relax. Mahek, he thinks he's a stud. In reality, his brain is the size of a peanut. Ignore him,' Kavya replied.

They had a good laugh and spent some time getting to know each other. Virat found that he was extremely similar to Mahek, personality-wise. They had the same taste in movies, food, sport etc. and even had the same attitude and perspective towards things. Though he was never too loud or outspoken, whenever he talked to Mehak, he would metamorphosize into a completely different person. The glow of her electric personality energized his brain as well as his heart.

It was time for the movie to begin, so they went inside the cinema hall and took their seats. The theatre was normally vacant on weekdays, and almost all the seats were unoccupied.

The movie turned out to be really boring and they soon

started to feel sleepy. Kavya saw a couple who were seated one row ahead of them and they were busy making their own movie. They were so engrossed in kissing each other that they hardly looked elsewhere. Both of them had closed their eyes and were feeling every inch of each other.

'Look at those dumbos,' Kavya whispered and continued, 'Virat, you should lend your flat on rent to such couples who are unable to find places to have sex.'

'Yeah, why not. I will even install a condom machine next to my door. Happy?' Virat said sarcastically to which Mehak smiled. This brought a smile to his face too. He felt like he was on top of the world.

'I think we should videotape them on our phone. What say, guys?' Kavya added.

'Have you lost it?' Virat said, annoyed.

'Awesome idea. It will be fun. Let's tease them later during the interval by showing them the video,' Mehak said excitedly.

Virat was shocked and felt trapped between the two girls. Earlier there was just Kavya, and now even Mehak had joined her troupe of crazy girls, it seemed. Mehak took her cell phone out and started recording them in the act. She angled the camera in such a way that both were clearly visible in the frame. The couple didn't have the slightest clue about what was happening. They got wilder with each passing minute and were almost on top of each other. Looking at them, all three started to laugh loudly.

'Hey, what are you doing? I will complain about you,' screamed someone from the back seat.

Mahek dropped the cell phone in fear and it rolled down a row.

'What are we doing? Look at them. We are just protesting,' Virat shouted to show that he was not afraid of the person who was threatening them.

But their luck was terrible because the guy actually went to the authorities and complained about the three of them and the racket they were creating. The authorities asked them to delete the video of the couple and threw everyone out of the hall.

'Don't you have a place to have sex, you assholes?' Kavya screamed on their way out.

'Should I book a room at a nearby hotel for the two of you?' Mehak added. She seemed to be having fun teasing them as well.

The trio ran to the parking lot towards Virat's car as the authorities were hot on their heels. They laughed thinking about how they got thrown out of the hall for shooting an MMS. Virat hadn't expected his first meeting with Mehak to turn out to be so adventurous.

As Virat drove the car, he kept checking out Mehak several times through the rear-view mirror. The smile on her face transported him to a dream world and her naughty eyes made him crazy for her. With each passing minute, he was falling for her more and more, while Mehak was drawing close to Virat and Kavya; she was starting to enjoy their company. When Virat had met her for the first time, he wasn't planning on falling in love. He wasn't even looking for another best friend. But she changed all that. Everything started with a little crush and slowly turned into something stronger. The attraction was electric and unexpected. She entered his world and turned it upside down. His mind tried to take control, but his heart would always win over the mind.

The next morning when Mehak reached college, she was slightly tensed as her assignments were incomplete. Kavya had finished writing Virat's assignment so he was in a relaxed frame of mind. When Mahek expressed her concern to the both of them, they laughed it off and told her about the plan some students had come up with.

'Are you serious?' Mehak asked.

'Yes, all the students who haven't finished the assignment have come up with a brilliant plan. So just relax and don't worry about the unfinished assignment,' Virat consoled her.

After the first lecture got over, some of the students left the class and went to the washroom. A few minutes later they returned with a sly smile on their faces.

'All set!' they screamed in unison.

Everyone was anxiously waiting to see what they had

planned. Virat, Mahek, and Kavya stared at each other, waiting for the big reveal. A few seconds later, there came a loud sound from the washroom. No one could mistake that sound—it was the sound of firecrackers burning! They had successfully trapped the professor in the washroom before he could come in for the next class. They knew he'd pay tribute to the 'Washroom Baba' before beginning the lecture. That's why they had named it 'baba' as it always came to their rescue in times of need. The caretaker ultimately helped the professor out who immediately rushed to the principal's room to complain about them. But by the time the principal could do something about it, the entire gang had run away. There was no other way to get hold of them. The submission of the assignment was forgotten in the entire process and Mehak sighed in relief.

Kavya had to leave early that day so Virat got an opportunity to spend some time alone with Mahek. They went to Mocha's for coffee where Virat shared his past with her—his family, past relationships—while Mahek told him about her ambitions in life. While Virat was perfectly comfortable talking to her about everything under the sun, he wasn't sure if Mehak was making small talk or if she too liked his company.

'So dancing is your passion?' Virat asked looking straight into her eyes. She silently nodded and turned her gaze away from him, breaking the temporary spell.

After a few seconds of silence, Virat added, 'Do you know

I have no knowledge of salsa? I joined because…'

Virat was about to complete his sentence when Mehak took his hand in hers and assured him that she would teach him everything she knew about salsa. He too tightened the grip on her hands and they looked straight into each other's eyes. Mahek immediately moved her hand away.

There's a famous saying that goes 'Don't try to understand a girl completely. If you do, then either you'll go mad or you'll start loving her.' Virat had started loving Mahek. She had stolen his heart before he could do something about it.

Shortly afterwards, Virat dropped her home and left for his apartment.

Once he reached the apartment, he sent her a message:

I had a great time with you. You're the reason I smile these days and I think I have found that someone who can make me have faith in love all again. Someone who can make me believe that even if things are hard in life, I don't have to worry as I have found that someone who can help me make it through. Someone who fills an empty space in my mind and heart. Someone who makes me feel complete. Someone who's enough for me. Someone who can accept me the way I am. Someone who is not insecure. I have been hurt so many times in the past that it takes a lot for me to trust someone now. The first time I saw you, I had this gut feeling that you and I were going to be together for a very long time. I hope I'm not irritating you with my silly talk, but I need to tell you that you are special. Thank you so much for coming into my life.

Once he sent the message, he kept the phone next to his laptop, waiting for her reply. But no message came. He scrolled through the pictures he had of her on his phone since he was missing every moment he had spent with her. He transferred them to his laptop and logged in to Gtalk. His chat-friend Rohan was online. It had been a few months since they first connected and both of them had become really good friends. Though Virat and Rohan had met only once, they talked with each other like they were childhood friends.

Virat: 'Hey. What's up? I need to tell you something.'

Rohan: 'Hi. Nothing much. Just sitting idle.'

Virat: 'Why, what happened? You know you can share anything with me.'

Rohan: 'Chuck it. You were going to tell me something…'

Virat: 'Dude, I think I am in love. I mean, I've never felt like this before. I just feel like gazing at her for hours. I sent a flirty message to her a few minutes back and am still waiting for her reply.'

Rohan: 'That's awesome, dude. So you've finally found the girl of your dreams after trying your luck with a dozen others.'

Virat: 'Ha ha! Fingers crossed. I hope it works out. How is life at your end? Anything troubling you? You don't seem your jolly self.'

Rohan: 'Nothing, yaar. My girlfriend is worried about our marriage and so we've been fighting every night.'

Virat: 'The couple that fights the most is the one most deeply in love. It shows that you care enough to notice that the other one screwed up, and care enough to mention it too.'

Rohan: 'It's not easy, beta. Now that you have fallen in love, you will realize it.'

Virat: 'Lol. I will resolve the fight in no time by being the first one to say sorry. Simple.'

Virat never shared things that were too personal with Rohan and it was the first time he had mustered the courage to tell him about what was happening in his love life. But before Rohan could respond to his message, his cousin entered the room and disconnected the internet. Virat too switched off his laptop and checked his mobile one last time before calling it a day. His eyes lit up seeing one message from Mahek.

'I love your company too. Kavya and you are full of life. See you tomorrow. Miss you.'

Virat started jumping on the bed with glee when he read the last two words—'Miss you'. Though the message was not overtly romantic or anything, he was happy because at least she had replied. He had never thought that he would meet someone as special as her. True love is a constant battle between the heart and the mind. Only when both are in sync with each other that true love comes into being. And Virat's mind and heart were both shouting only one name in chorus. He lay on the couch trying to imagine her next to him. He was so excited that he was unable to figure out what to do next. If Kavya wouldn't have warned him, he would have asked her out right away. He wanted to tell Kavya about the message but it was quite late and she would be asleep by then. He switched his laptop back on to check whether Rohan was online or not. He wasn't either. He went to sleep that night with a smile on his face.

Dhuaa

Rohan was chatting with Virat casually in his room while also thinking about his own complicated love life. He was about to take a sip of his coffee when I opened the door to his bedroom.

'Hey buddy,' I shouted.

'Aditya, when did you come?' Rohan asked.

'This evening with Mom. She had some work here, so we finished that and came straight to your place. Mom is outside discussing something with Aunty. Hurry up. Let's go out.'

'Just give me a minute. I'm chatting with my friend Virat,' Rohan stated.

Before he could chat again, I removed the internet plug and switched off his computer.

'What is this? I have come to fucking meet you and you are on the internet. Let's go to our favourite spot,' I said pulling him from his chair.

'You wanna go to Anna? Have you taken permission?' asked.

I nodded and shut down his laptop before he could start again. Though it was drizzling a bit, Rohan raced his bike towards Anna. Anna was our favourite tea stall where we'd catch up over steaming hot cups of tea and pakoras.

Rohan was a shy and reserved boy who kept mostly to himself. His family was the orthodox kinds and not very outgoing. The one thing Rohan did love was going to the gym. He was a typical gym freak who worked hard day and night to get great biceps. He was well mannered and was always very well turned out. This made him a favourite among girls who liked silent, brooding type of men. He was very bad at telling a lie because the innocence in his eyes would give the lie away. He was extremely caring and believed that not displaying affection openly showed that you are ashamed of who you're with. Inspired by Bollywood movies, he was overtly romantic and loved to go out for candlelight dinners with his girlfriend. He was slightly superstitious and used to wear precious stone rings on his fingers to ward off evil and control his temper. More importantly, he was focused on achieving his goals and was confident about achieving his dreams, one of them being helping orphan kids.

'Here comes your cup of tea. Do you want a smoke too?' I asked Rohan taking out a ciggie from my pocket and lighting it.

'No, it's ok,' he replied.

'Don't you get bored typing so much on Gtalk?' I asked him out of curiosity. I personally hated it.

'I don't talk much. It's just that my friend Virat was online and he was telling me about his love-life, so I couldn't log off,' Rohan added.

'Oh, cool. Who is he?'

Rohan told me how he and Virat were online friends who met each other through a blogger's site some time back and then added each other on Gtalk. They had met once when Virat wanted some information regarding a particular orphanage. Rohan had all the details about the orphanage as it was his dream to work for them and thus he had met Virat to help him. Though Rohan was an introvert and shied away from making friends online, he was never wrong at judging people's intentions. He found Virat to be very genuine and decided to help him out. They've been friends ever since.

'At this age, guys go online to make girlfriends and here you have found a guy online. You are on the right track brother,' I laughed.

'Shut up, Adi.'

'I mean it, seriously. One of my friends is dating a girl he has never met. At least you've met your guy once,' I added teasingly.

'Trust me. He is a nice guy. We are not that close, but we're good friends.'

'Ok, boss. I trust you. So, how's life in Pune?' I asked.

'Just routine. You know what, I'm lucky to have a brother like you. In today's time we can manage to make good friends with whom we can go out and have fun, but it is difficult to have a brother who can understand you and really sit down and listen to you. I love you, Adi,' Rohan said sounding senti all of a sudden.

'Are you sure you're drinking tea or it is it bhaang?'

'Fuck off, yaar. I'm serious,' he said getting annoyed.

Rohan was my cousin who stayed in Pune at NIBM and we were friends more than brothers. There was nothing hidden between us and he was the only one in the family who knew everything about me. Similarly, even he never kept any secrets from me. I had many relatives in Pune and Rohan was one of them. Whenever I got a chance to visit Pune, I'd make sure I meet him. I always felt comfortable with him and Rohan too liked discussing his life with me alone, though he had other cousins too. He never liked talking about personal stuff with other members of his family.

'How is Zoya? Is everything all right now between you two?' I asked. The last I spoke with him, he had told me about the issues he was facing with his current girlfriend.

'Things are getting worse. I have planned something for her to surprise her but don't know if it'll work. I should have realized that inter-caste relationships are not easy.'

'Don't worry. Chill. And how is your sexy French teacher? Are you still taking classes from her?'

'Yes, we are more like friends and she knows about my love life as well. She is the one I share everything with in your absence,' he answered.

'Does she still show interest in you?' I asked with curiosity. Rohan had mentioned once that she liked him.

Rohan had completed his BA from Wadia College and had joined a reputed company recently. He had a passion to learn French and wanted to Major in the language. Thus he had decided to take special classes in his free time to learn French which is where he met the teacher who took a sudden liking to him.

'I think so. She is a couple of years older than me. How does it matter anyway? I love Zoya,' Rohan replied.

'You are seriously lucky. An older woman lusting after you. Gosh, I have always fantasized about my teachers having a crush on me, but they always threw me out of their classes instead,' I winked.

After talking for some time, we left and went back home. Everyone always asks me how Rohan and I gel so well with each other, and I say to them 'We just understand each other.' There were times when we both wouldn't say anything to each other but knew what we needed. We would talk every night on the phone and my mom would end up asking how we always had so much to say to each other. I'd always tell her 'We are best friends, not brothers.' Family has nothing to do with blood. Family is the people you love and the people who count on you and love you right back. I loved Rohan and he counted on me.

I decided to stay back in Pune for a few days. I needed a change from my hectic life. Rohan and I ended up missing a family function just to hang out together. We needed a reason to skip it anyway, and hanging out together seemed like the best one. So, we decided to chill and enjoy our time together at 'Dhuaa'. The place served one of the best hookahs in the city. It had an amazing ambience and the beautiful rooftop view of the city was utter perfection. We ordered 'Jannat Hookah' that had a special base of vodka and whiskey.

'You want to order starters?' I asked Rohan once our Hookah was served.

'Let's order some Pattaya?'

Pattaya was his favourite dish—a Malaysian dish made by wrapping chicken fried rice in fried egg. Rohan inhaled the drags of smoke one after the other, excitedly, and felt a little tipsy after sometime because of the alcohol base of the hookah.

'You are acting like a guy who, upon seeing a naked girl after years, pounces on her instantly and climaxes within minutes. You're only human, Rohan, so enjoy the foreplay, the flavour,' I teased snatching the pipe from him.

'I am just bit upset because of Zoya. I'm confused if I should let her go or hold on to her,' he added.

'Let time decide. You don't have to think about it. Nothing's in our hands. Ultimately the person who is meant to be with you will stay and the rest will leave, in their own time,' I said trying to console him.

'I hope the surprise date that I have planned for her changes her decision of moving on.'

'Take it easy, Rohan. I mean, go slow on the hookah. It will be difficult to handle you later,' I joked to lighten up his mood. We soon left for Rohan's house.

Due to the family get together, everyone had gone to our farmhouse in Baner, so there'd be only the two of us in his house at night. I was partially happy about that since I would not have to worry about getting Rohan home so drunk, even though Rohan was having difficulty to walk even a few metres by himself.

Somehow I managed to drag Rohan out of Dhuaa in his intoxicated state. We searched for an auto as we had no other mode of conveyance. His parents had taken the car with them, and he had left his bike at the service centre. I had always hated public transport facilities in Pune and that night was no different. No one was ready to come to NIBM area and with no options left, we started walking to his home. Rohan kept his hands around my shoulder and was walking with my support. Suddenly, a gang of girls on bikes slowed down near us and started passing lewd comments.

'Champu, are you both gay?' one of the girls shouted.

I couldn't see their faces as they had scarves covering it—typical Punekar biker style. When I turned towards Rohan, I realized why they were teasing us. Rohan was leaning on my shoulder, and it almost looked like he was kissing me. By the time I shifted Rohan's weight on my other shoulder, an auto stopped beside us. Without telling him where to go, we both sat inside and told the driver to drive straight. The girls disappeared after a few seconds.

'Rohan yaar. You embarrassed me in front of the hot chicks! Behave, you asshole,' I shouted.

'What did I do? I was just resting my head because of the terrible headache I have,' Rohan muttered.

Dammit. Do you realize how hot they were? Your drunkenness has cost me a chance to score with them. They looked so ravishing in those tiny shorts. We could have…'

I was about to complete my statement when the gang appeared again and started passing the same comments. Rohan was again leaning on my shoulder the way a girlfriend leans on her boyfriend.

'You both look like you're made for each other. You can continue romancing. We are not looking at you,' one of them shouted and they all started laughing loudly.

Rohan looked at them but didn't react.

'If they're so interested in our love-life, ask them to join us and we can have a group-some! ' I whispered in Rohan's ears.

Rohan, clearly not in his senses, asked them if they were interested in joining us.

'No, we're not gay like you,' one girl in teeny-tiny shorts replied.

I couldn't control my laughter any longer. I knew they would tease him more and that's why I provoked him to tease them as well. The trick worked and soon the girls left us to our misery. Rohan started insisting I drop him off at his French tutor's house. I tried to calm him down and change his mind, but he kept insisting, saying that he would be back in an hour. I took the house keys from him and dropped him at his tutor's apartment which was not that far from his place. I waited in the auto till Rohan entered her apartment. Once he did, I left.

Her apartment was on the second floor. Rohan rang the bell to her apartment a couple of times.

'Riddhima, it's me, Rohan. Open the door.'

'Coming! Just hold on for a second,' Riddhima shouted from the kitchen.

After completing her education in Pune, Riddhima had chosen to stay in the city that she had grown to love over the years. She taught French in her free time. She was short, with a wheatish complexion and sharp, bright eyes. With her amazing way of speaking and great presence of mind, she could win anyone's heart. She always lived for the moment and believed 'Unplanned moments are always better than planned ones'. Her short hair suited her personality and her perfect curves made her look amazing, no matter what she wore. She had a tattoo on her upper back that give her an edgy look. She was an independent girl who would spend hours wearing makeup. She also loved wearing junk jewellery. She had been teaching Rohan for quite some time now and since they belonged to the same age group, they just clicked. She treated Rohan more as a friend than a student. Somewhere in the corner of her heart, she had developed feelings for Rohan despite knowing that he loved Zoya. However, she kept her hopes up as she was also aware of the complications in Rohan and Zoya's relationship.

'Rohan, what are you doing here so late ?' she asked.

'Nothing. I have a terrible headache.'

Rohan was so drunk that he almost lost his balance. Riddhima helped him sit on the sofa.

'Are you drunk?' she asked just to confirm.

'No. I tried hookah with a liquor base. I am feeling a little tipsy, that's all. I am really ok,' he answered.

'You said that your cousin Aditya was in town. Where is he now?' She was still confused by Rohan's unexpected visit.

'Yeah, I was with him. He dropped me here and went back home,' Rohan said trying to regain his senses.

'So why aren't you going home? You parents must be worried about you, Rohan,' she said in concern.

'Don't worry, they are not at home. I will go back in a while. I'm meeting Zoya tomorrow,' Rohan stammered.

He rested his head on Riddhima's shoulder and kept repeating Zoya's name as he slowly dozed off to sleep. The closeness made Riddhima feel a bit uncomfortable. She gently put his head down on the sofa while running her fingers through his hair. She felt an urge to hug him back and to continue doing so the entire night. She wished he would utter her name instead of Zoya's, and make love to her, but that clearly wasn't going to happen. Somehow, she managed to keep a check on her emotions. She wished they were dating but knew that he liked someone else. She thought that she was the right one for him. Sadly, some people are meant to fall in love and even meant to be together, but not as couples. Only as friends.

It's Hard to Let Go

'Rohan, your cell has been vibrating since ages. Get up sleepyhead; it's eight in the morning!' Riddhima screamed holding a cup of coffee in her hand.

'Riddhi…you…I slept here? Oh God! Aditya must be so worried about me,' Rohan said jumping out of the bed.

He had spent the night at Riddhima's home, unable to recall anything about the previous night. Riddhima reminded him that he had to meet Zoya. Rohan rushed out of her house without drinking the cup of coffee she had made for him.

I was fast asleep in Rohan's bedroom when he suddenly entered and quickly latched the door behind him.

'What the fuck? Is this the time to come home? Bastard, you told me that you were dating Zoya, and now here you are, coming back after spending the night at Riddhima's home!' I screamed.

'Shut up, Adi. I will explain everything to you later. And

yes, I am still dating Zoya, and I'm going to spend the entire day with her today. Do you have a problem with that?' he said recklessly and hurriedly left to take a shower.

Within minutes, he was dressed. He took his bag and tiptoed to the exit door. I was worried because I knew I'd be the one in trouble. No excuse sounded good enough.

'What am I going to tell your parents? They reached at dawn, so they are fast asleep at the minute,' I said in a hushed tone, afraid the noise would wake up our parents.

'Oh, thank God. That means the car is back. I was worried I'd have to take the auto again. Tell them anything you wish. I am leaving. Bye.'

Saying that he left. I looked at him leave and broke into a huge smile, because it was exactly the thing I would've done had I been in his place. After all, you tend to act stupid when you're in love. There are three things a person needs to be happy: work, friends, and somebody to love. Rohan was fighting for the third one. The love of his life, Zoya!

Zoya was a simple girl hailing from a conservative Muslim family in Pune. She had been in a relationship with Rohan for almost a year now. She was tall, fair, with black eyes that were always outlined with dark kohl. She looked extremely cute with her nose ring and jhumkaas. She had a flawless skin that anyone could gaze at for hours without blinking.

She preferred wearing Indian clothes, and salwar-kameez was her favourite choice of outfit. She looked pretty elegant in one as well. She was not a regular city girl who spent too much time bothering about her looks. The simplicity in her thoughts made her different from the rest. Her dimpled smile drove guys crazy and Rohan would constantly tease her that if their children didn't get the same dimples, he would divorce her. She was a regular blood donor and wanted to work for a NGO.

Her family was against love marriage and especially against an inter-caste one. Hence, she decided to hit the brakes on her relationship with Rohan even though she loved him. It was a big day for Rohan as he wanted to convince Zoya to change her decision and fight for their relationship. He picked Zoya up from the main highway. She looked cute in her white salwar-kameez. She wore the earrings Rohan had given her on her birthday.

'Where are we going?' she asked in her mesmeric voice.

'Shush. You are not going to ask any questions today. You are just going to enjoy our date,' Rohan smiled looking at her and kissed her hand. They both took their respective seats and Rohan soon drove away to the outskirts of Pune.

' Anything special today?' she asked again.

'How is it possible for someone to be this cute? You are, seriously, one cute baby. I love you so much,' said Rohan pulling her cheeks as she leaned on him.

Rohan had planned to spend some time with Zoya at

Tiger Point in Lonavla. He had even planned a few surprises for her just to make her feel special. As they reached the express highway, he played soft music and asked her to open the box kept on the dashboard.

'What is this?' she asked in amazement.

'Open it. It's full of love. I know I don't need to prove my love but I just wanted to express it to you this one time.'

She opened it to find a letter hidden inside. A letter written on a red paper that was shaped like a rose petal. She glanced at Rohan once and started reading it.

I love you. Ever since you came into my life, I've looked forward to each day—watching the early morning sunrise with you in my bed, dozing off under the dark blue skies, beneath a zillion stars. You make me feel as no one else does. I like the person I am when I'm with you. You bring out a part of me that I never knew existed. You made me turn into a better person. I now have a reason to live; a cause, a reason to believe in all the wonderful moments in life. You took my heart away and turned me into an ocean of love, and you saw in me all the qualities that no one else could ever see. You gave me respect, love, care, and peace. Yes, I love you, for all these special qualities and so much more. I love you for being yourself, and I love you because of the person you made me. Please, be with me forever. As long as you are by my side, I can fight the whole world but I can't stand to be alone. I love you, Zoya. I really do.

Zoya had tears in her eyes. She tumed her gaze away to avoid eye contact with Rohan. She felt helpless and wanted to run away, leaving everything else behind her, but couldn't. Rohan held her hand and tumed her around to face him. It takes a minute to like someone but it takes a lifetime to forget someone. It was not easy for Zoya to live like this.

'Rohan, can I ask you something?' she asked.

Rohan nodded.

'You think I'll be able to live happily without you?' she said as tear rolled down her cheek.

'Zoya, I know you can't. I know that you really love me. That's why I am asking you to hold on. I've always wanted to tell you that you have changed my life. I have started noticing the happiness that exists around me. I really don't know how or when you became this huge part of my life, but I do know that I want to be with you, forever.'

Silence filled the air and both of them remained quiet, holding hands until they reached Tiger point. Rohan parked his car and made Zoya sit on the bonnet. He sat beside her and placed his head on her shoulder.

'It's so pleasant here. Thank you for making my day so special,' Zoya smiled.

'I have another surprise for you,' Rohan said as he came down to retrieve his laptop that was kept on the back seat.

Climbing back on the bonnet again, he played a video that he had made especially for her. The video was a montage of their pictures while her favourite song 'Tum ho toh gaata hai dil' played in the background. A few lines appeared on the screen at the end of the video.

Jahan yaad na aaye teri,
Woh tanhaai kis kaam ki.
Bigde rishte na bane,
To khudaai kis kaam ki.
Beshak apni manzil tak jaana hai hamein,
Lekin jahaan se apne na dikhein,
Woh oonchaai kis kaam ki!

Each photograph of theirs made her smile. She got nostalgic about all the good times they had spent together in the past one year. These few minutes had revived all those past memories. She was speechless and wanted to freeze that moment. She didn't know what life had in store for her; she just wanted to tell the world how much she loved Rohan.

When we are in love, it feels like it will last forever. We put all our trust in the person we are in love with and share our darkest secrets with them too. But there comes a time when you have to take a decision against your choice, even when no one is at fault.

The most difficult thing to explain in life is the simplest truth called love. Zoya was not able to express her emotions but she, too, cried from within.

'Rohan, it's not working anymore. I don't want to go against my parents and we should have thought about it long back. It would be better if we stopped everything now. It's not easy for me either, but it's the only option I have left,' Zoya cried.

'We can handle this, Zoya. Please, be patient. We will make them understand and tell them about us. Everyone will approve,' Rohan pleaded with her.

'No, Rohan. It's not possible. You know how my family is. They are very conservative and they will never approve of our relationship. I thought about it a few days back when I heard Abbu talking about my marriage and he got angry when my mom requested him to ask for my approval first.

'Please, Zoya. Don't give up like this. We should give it another shot. It's better than regretting it our entire lives,' Rohan said with tears in his eyes.

'Why don't you understand? I am already so tense; please don't make me weaker. You are my strength and you must always smile. I talked to your sister and she agrees with me, too.

'When did you talk to her?'

'A few days back, post my discussion with Abbu about our marriage.'

Rohan tried to make her understand that everything would work out if they both stayed firm on their decision, but Zoya didn't have the courage to go against her family. Rohan stopped the conversation short and bought some Pakodas for them. To lighten the mood, he told her about what had happened the night before. She managed to smile.

Rohan continuously checked the time on his watch, waiting for the right moment to surprise her, one last time.

He kept his fingers crossed and a few minutes later, Zoya received the final surprise of the day. She received a text message on her mobile from Rohan. He had sent her a message through an online SMS site. Zoya was surprised to receive the sudden text message and started reading it aloud,

> *When I met you, I thought it would last forever. I never thought that there would l be a moment in our lives when we would part ways. I know you love me and really care about me. I know you want me to smile even when you're no longer by my side. I know you want me to enjoy my life even when you won't be with me. I know that you want me to always take care of myself. Ok, I will. I will do everything that you want me to. I promise. I won't hurt myself. I will eat my food on time and even sleep on time. But it's not just about me, sweetheart. I assure you that I will do everything that you want, but can you give me the same assurance? I know that this our last date, probably...*

Zoya put the phone away. She did not have the courage to read any further. There were tears streaming down her cheeks. She kept her mobile inside and hugged Rohan. They were so engrossed in hugging each other that they didn't even realize that it had started to rain. Each raindrop that fell on them brought them closer and Zoya was able to hide her tears behind the raindrops. They hugged like there was no tomorrow. Probably even their soul could feel that it would be their last touch. It started raining heavily but Rohan and Zoya didn't move an inch from the bonnet of the car. Resting their back on the glass, they made love to each other, one last time.

Rohan dropped Zoya home in the evening and requested her to think over her decision once more. Though she agreed, somehow he knew that it was over. But as always, his heart ruled over his brain and even the thought of living a life without her made him shiver. He was not ready to accept it, and entertained the fantasies of things somehow working out. He saw a hidden glimmer of hope somewhere though he had a clear indication it was over.

'Nothing seems to be working anymore,' Rohan said as he reached home.

'If you are not meant to be together then it's not going to work. I know it's easy to say all this but that's the fact, and you can't change it,' I said trying to make him understand.

'For the first time I've known what it feels like to love someone. I know Riddhima has feelings for me too. But I somehow want to be with Zoya though it seems like a distant possibility now. But I don't want to give up on Zoya so easily.'

'Look Rohan, you can't force someone to love you, and

by forcing, you don't prove your love, you prove that you are weak and immature. So don't behave like one.'

I knew it was not easy to forget someone so easily. I had gone through a similar situation in my life as well. It doesn't matter how long you were together, the mere thought of being alone leads to depression and a feeling of hopelessness encloses you. Strange is the world of love where you find so many reasons to keep going, yet you choose to avoid listening to your heart and just one reason is reason enough to move on.

Rohan logged on to his Gtalk once I went to sleep. He wanted someone with whom he could share his pain. More than that, he needed that one person who could support him in his decision to not let go. He felt Virat was the one who would understand him well as he was waiting for his relationship to click. They greeted each other and started chatting.

Rohan: 'I am losing the love of my life, slowly and painfully. You are lucky, my friend, that you have your best friend and your love by your side.'

Virat: 'Don't be so sad. You are not losing anything. It's her loss that she is going away from you. And keep your hopes alive. Who knows, maybe she will change her mind?'

Rohan: 'I don't know. I am totally confused. I understand that going against your family is not easy but somewhere I feel there is some other reason behind it. I can somehow sense it.'

Virat: 'Relax. And never say that you are alone. I remember you mentioning something about your teacher who understands your feelings, right? '

Rohan: 'Riddhima. Yeah, she does. She really supports me and is really sweet.'

Virat: 'See, you have an option. Don't worry. Just chill. Plus you have me to count on as well. If you need anything or if you feel alone, just buzz me. I will be there.'

Rohan: 'Thanks. What's happening with you?'

Virat: 'Dude, I have my dance competition coming up and I am super tense as I am the Shakti Kapoor of dancing.'

Rohan: 'Ha ha. Best of luck bro.'

Rohan logged out just when he received a call from Riddhima. She was worried about him and had called to see how he was doing. She wanted things to get back to normal between Rohan and Zoya as she wanted to see Rohan happy and his happiness lied in Zoya. When she came to know what had happened, she tried to lift his morale by telling him she'll be by his side, come what may.

'Rohan, I know this is not the right time to tell you this but I really care about you and can't see you like this. Smile for me, at least. Whenever you feel low, you will always find me holding your hand and walking with you,' Riddhima said expressing her feelings.

'I know and I am lucky to have you with me. I hope my life gets back on track soon. Love you for whatever you are doing for me,' Rohan said emotionally and hung up.

Riddhima prayed for Rohan's well-being and happiness.

Love surprises us in unexpected ways, in ways that are beyond our comprehension. It's never the sweet words or the mushy gifts that matter. What matters more are little things like caring about someone and not being able to sleep till you're sure that the one you love is safe and sound. On one side, there was Riddhima who really loved Rohan and wanted to live her life with him, and on the other hand there was Zoya who really loved Rohan but had ruined every possibility of a future with him. Rohan was lonely and felt alone even when there were two girls in his life who really loved him. He cared about Zoya and trusted her completely. But he knew that when you completely trust a person with all your heart, you either get a friend for life or a lesson for life!

Then, there was Virat who loved Mahek and wanted to spend his entire life with her and there was Kavya who always stood by his side and was a really good friend to him. Rohan and Virat were not exactly the closest of friends, but knew that they had each other's backs. A relationship does not need promises, terms, and conditions. It just needs two wonderful people that click!

Life is Not Always Fair

Mid-August, 2009

The dance competition at Biosis College was inching closer to its date. Mehak would've never agreed to dance with Virat if it wasn't for the fun they had been having lately. She knew that he wasn't really interested in the dance competition, yet she decided to teach him the basics and teamed up with him. Solo dance is comparatively easier compared to group dancing as it doesn't require co-ordination between two people and some mistakes can be overlooked. But in salsa, it was unacceptable for them to make even a minute error. Mahek wanted to win this competition because it would've helped her move a step closer to fulfilling her dream. She was tense as the competition was hardly a few days away and Virat was still not getting the moves right.

Mahek used to teach Virat salsa daily and they would

practice endlessly to get the moves right at Virat's apartment. With each passing day, his dancing improved but the chemistry between them was lacking as Virat was focusing more on the legs than the eyes. It had to be effortless dancing but it seemed as though he was 'forcing' his legs to move back and forth and he always had trouble knowing when to pause. Virat always made a mistake around beat four when he was supposed to pause.

'Virat, how many times have I told you to let your body loose while dancing? Don't be stiff. You keep committing the same mistake all over again and you are not concentrating on the pauses,' Mehak said irritably.

'What sort of a stupid dance form is this? Let me teach you the Nashik dhol dance. There are no pauses in it,' said Virat.

'Classy people learn salsa while others do the naagin dance,' she shot back at him.

'Oh, please. Anyway, chuck it. Let's practice,' Virat said, keeping his hands on her waist.

'Move your right foot first. Imagine where you are standing as point 1, then point 2 is about a foot in front of you, and point 3 is about a foot behind you. Now move, rhythmically,' Mahek guided him as their eyes met.

They came closer as they danced to the point that they were almost touching each other. Their faces were so close that their lips almost met as well. Virat held her firmly by her waist and brought her even closer. He could feel her breath on his neck. Virat was about to lean in and kiss her when the bell rang. Mehak regained her composure and pushed Virat away while his heart skipped a beat, the way it does when someone catches you watching porn.

Virat opened the door to find Kavya standing in front of him.

'Kavya, you should have messaged me before coming,' Virat screamed.

'Shut up. I am not here to meet you. I have come to meet Mahek. Where is she?' she said walking inside the bedroom and continued, 'Oh, there you are! Mehak, I just asked the organizers when your is act. They told me you both will be performing third.'

Mehak's nervousness was clearly visible on her face. She was almost on the verge of crying because she knew how desperately she wanted to win the competition. Virat could sense her tension and see the tears in her eyes as they stood there, staring at each other. He went closer to her and gave her a pat on the back, assuring her that they would win the competition, easily. He decided to get serious about winning the competition since it mattered so much to her.

'Do you want to something to eat?' Virat asked both of them.

'What all do you have? I am really hungry,' Kavya replied.

'Oh, madam. This is not a hotel. It's my house.'

'Can you make Egg Bhurji for me?' Mehak said in a sweet voice.

'Yeah, yeah. He will. He is an awesome cook. You should taste him. I mean something made by him,' Kavya teased.

Virat threw a pillow at her as he walked into the kitchen. Mehak looked down in awkwardness. As Kavya lay down on the bed, she noticed that Virat had cleaned his room and everything was in its place. Kavya thought it odd as she had seen his room clean for the first time in her life. She was surprised to see this sudden change in him. She never missed an opportunity to pull his leg and now she would tease him all the more since she had the upper hand knowing Virat would keep his mouth sealed in front of Mahek.

'Mahek, you should have seen this room a few days back. It looked so sexy,' Kavya said in a high pitch, making sure Virat heard her.

'Will you keep your mouth shut?' Virat shouted from inside.

Mahek was curious to know more and kept asking her how the room looked. Virat tried hard to keep her quiet but to no avail.

'This rope that's hanging above your head was previously being used to dry his underwear and dirty towels,' Kavya laughed.

'Ewww,' Mahek said making a face while Virat ran to the kitchen saying 'Fuck off'.

They both started to tease him endlessly. Kavya gave fuel to fire by adding that the undergarments had holes in them. Mahek and Kavya were rolling on the floor with laughter, making fun of Virat. He was still in the kitchen listening to all the comments that both the girls were passing. He couldn't take it anymore. The Egg Bhurji was ready and so was Virat. Instead of bringing plates from the kitchen, he brought a bucket of cold water from the washroom and spilled it on both of them.

'What the fuck! Are you crazy? I am not going to spare you now,' Kavya added and ran towards him to take revenge.

He ran into the hall where Kavya followed him while Mehak connected the pipe from the washroom and splashed water on him.

'Ok, stop! I'm sorry. Stop it. The electronic items will get wet,' Virat pleaded with both the girls pointing to his TV and speakers.

Mahek shut the tap, worried that they'd alarm the neighbour with their screaming and yelling. They took a deep breath and everyone smiled looking at each other. They eventually cleared the mess that they had created and changed into Virat's clothes. Virat served them the Bhurji and turned on the television .

'How's it?' he asked looking at the girls.

'It's yummy. I love the way it tastes. We get a similar tasting Bhurji at some place on FC road. I am crazy about it,' Mehak said licking her fingers.

'It's seriously good,' Kavya added.

Virat glanced at Mahek and caught her looking back at him. He was pleased to know that she liked his cooking.

They exchanged smiles with each other. There was something that held them together. Something that made them better together. Something that made them more than just friends.

But with all the fun that the trio had together, somewhere in their minds, there was also the pressure of winning the competition. Virat decided that he would take the competition seriously for the entire week and practice hard so that Mahek could reach closer to her dream. Her dream and passion was his now.

When you set your heart on something and put all your efforts into making your dream turn into a reality, nothing can stop you from achieving it. Virat practiced hard the entire week as he knew how important the win was to Mahek. With each passing day, he even mastered the foot movements and his pauses perfectly. It wasn't surprising that with each passing day Virat and Mahek not only coordinated well physically, they were connected in their minds too. You meet a person and instantly know that you're going to be best friends with that person. Just because you're a grown up doesn't mean that you don't need someone to confide in. In fact, amid the complexities of life, you need that special person to share your life with. But the important thing to remember is that there should be a sense of mutual respect and indefinite care for each other.

Just the thought of asking her to be a part of his life made him shiver. Moreover, due to Mahek's nervousness, even Virat was feeling uneasy. The competition was hardly a day away and the pressure of performing well and winning made him nervous. He feared that if they lost the competition, he may lose Mahek forever. He feared that if they didn't perform well, Mahek would stop talking to him and they will cease to be even friends. He feared Mahek would end up regretting letting him dance with her.

This fear and the nervousness made him take a drastic step. He made up his mind to meet with the seniors who were competing with them. He didn't know them personally, but thought of interacting with them once before the competition. His big idea was to plead with them one night before to let them win. At that point, he was willing to do anything to win the competition as well as Mahek's heart.

After dinner, he went to college alone without informing Kavya and Mehak about his plan. If he would have disclosed his plan to them, they would have never allowed him to proceed with it. Hence, he decided to go alone to the college auditorium where the seniors were practicing. With heavy steps, he walked towards the stage where a group of students were practicing their moves to the beats of the music. He stopped at the main door to the auditorium and thought once again whether he was doing the right thing or not, but his mind had taken over and he couldn't think of any other way of winning this competition than plead with them.

He was ready to pay any price for it. He walked through the darkness of the corridor and entered the auditorium. The main lights were on and there were a couple of groups who were practicing on stage. Some other students were just standing about and watching them dance. He walked towards them with shivering legs. He was brave enough to have a talk with them, but was afraid about the outcome. What if they didn't agree? What if they told Mahek about his little stunt? He made his mind up; it was now or never.

'Yes, you there, mister. Any problem?' one of them asked Virat as he stood looking clueless in front of everyone.

'I wanted to confess something… I need a favour,' Virat stammered.

'What favour?'one of the girls asked.

There were around four girls and five guys in front of him out of which a couple of them were practicing while the others were seated,

'I'm in love with a girl and I need to win the salsa competition for her,' Virat stated, avoiding all eye contact with them.

'So how can we help you?'

'I want you to lose tomorrow and I'm ready to do anything in return. Whatever you ask for. But let me win tomorrow. I really love her and I can't live without her. Please, For you it is just a competition but for me it is…'

Before Virat could finish the sentence, he received a huge blow on his face from one of the guys. The next moment

Virat was lying on the floor, bleeding from his lips.

'Why are you...I am just requesting...Did I...' he stammered.

No sooner had he managed to get up that he received another punch from the other guy, but this time it was on his chest. The guy hit him so hard that he fell crashing on the floor.

'You're trying to act smart, haan? Bloody loser. You want us to lose in front of you? You don't have the guts to prove your love by winning and you want us to lose for you. Ha ha,' one of the guys shouted post kicking him in the stomach.

'Fuck off, you cheapo,' the girl screamed and asked him to get lost.

Everyone teased him and made fun of him. No one would have ever agreed to lose, no matter how much he pestered. One of the students was kind enough to get him some water. Virat refused and left the auditorium, wounded and weak. With each lie that you come up with, you change the nature of your relationship. Virat had not only lied to his love but even to his best friend, and now he felt nothing but heartbroken and guilty. After practicing so hard for a week, he should have trusted himself and his dancing capability. He shouldn't have gone so far as to plead with the other contestants, but the fear of losing the love of his life had made him lose his mind.

It was D-day and Biosis College was all set for a dance competition. One could sense the excitement that filled the entire auditorium and everyone was ready to set the stage on fire. Kavya was waiting for Virat and Mahek, arranging their costumes and taking care of other small things. She was equally nervous as she knew both of them had put a lot of effort in preparing for the competition. She called Virat to confirm whether he had left for college or not.

'I am reaching in 10 minutes,' Virat said and disconnected the call.

He was worried because of the drama that had happened last night. He just hoped that all those present during the incident had kept their mouth shut and didn't go around gossiping about it. After returning home last night, he was not able to sleep and kept thinking about what he had done in a fit of panic and nervousness. Somehow, he regained his lost confidence because it was a matter of his self-respect, dignity, and ego. He wanted to win this not only for Mahek but to prove that he was not a 'cheapo' as the girl had called him. He reached college and went straight backstage.

'What happened to you?' Kavya asked in a state of shock when she saw the cuts on Virat's lips.

'Nothing, just...'

'You got into a fight with someone? Tell me the truth, Virat,' she shouted in concern.

'I will tell you later. Where is Mahek?' Virat said trying to locate her.

'She has not reached yet,' Kavya replied.

Kavya could sense something fishy but didn't bother Virat too much so he remains focused on his performance. The show had begun but still there were no sign of Mehak. This worried her more. She asked her other friends and even some professors about her whereabouts but no one seemed to know where she was. Even her mobile phone was switched off. Virat searched for her in the entire campus but couldn't trace her anywhere. The first performers were already done and the second group came on stage. Luck favoured them as the judges announced they were going to take a short break after the second performance. This bought them some more time to locate Mehak.

'She must be stuck in traffic, it seems,' Virat comforted Kavya who was getting more furious with each passing minute.

'Virat, something is wrong. Tell me what happened. Where is Mehak? Is she alright? Did anything happen to her last night?' Kavya panicked.

'It would be better if we looked for her rather than discussing about what happened yesterday. Do you have her parent's numbers?' Virat asked.

'No, I don't have their number. Wait, let me talk to the judges and see if they can reschedule our performance by giving us a new time slot.'

Kavya went to talk to the judges but despite trying her best, she failed to convince them. 'You don't get such opportunities everyday, and if you can't make the most of it, then I'm sorry, you don't even deserve to be here. I pity you, beta, but there's nothing we can do,' said one of the judges.

Kavya returned with a sad look on her face. Virat was still trying to convince the judges, making excuses, but to no use. You always realize the value of something after you lose it. Virat couldn't digest the fact that it was going to end this way. Mehak and Virat had grown close because of the dance competition and now the reason he had taken up dance in the first place was nowhere to be found. Kavya couldn't believe Mehak didn't turn up for such an important performance. It was her dream to get selected and she simply couldn't fathom why Mehak didn't show up. Virat felt guilty as he thought that they guys he took a panga with had done something to her. His one bad decision had screwed up their happiness.

There are times when you feel nothing good could possibly come your way. When dreams are shattered and you feel a void inside, you are rendered empty and hopeless. You try so hard to get past the emptiness that you know inside your soul that there is no way out. It's said that one should always follow his heart. But what if it leads you to a dead end?

Your Flaws Are Perfect

'Oh, cheapo! What happened to your love partner? She dumped you after getting to know what a jerk you were last night?' the same girl from that group teased him as Virat and Kavya walked through the corridor.

'No, She must've been really stressed out after those long hours of practice.'

The girl and her gang of friends continued passing comments till Virat left the campus. Virat tried to avoid eye contact with anyone. He still hadn't gotten over last night's episode.

Kavya was furious but didn't say a word because she knew that Virat was hiding something. The only person she was concerned about at that point was Mahek. Her mobile phone was still switched off. Kavya walked alongside Virat who was lost in his thoughts completely. He picked up his phone and messaged Mahek:

Call me as soon as you read this message.

After walking a mile, Virat sat on a bench along the footpath. Kavya looked at him and saw tears rolling down his eyes.

'What's wrong, Virat? Are you okay?' she asked.

Virat looked at her with a guilty look on his face and told her about what had happened last night. He narrated everything that he had gone through and also confessed that though it was wrong on his part, he didn't tell anyone about it. He had no idea where she was and the last time he had talked with her was last evening. He had messaged her before sleeping but she didn't reply. Kavya was shocked hearing this and almost pulled her hair out in frustration. She was unable to understand why Virat had taken such a drastic step and ended up shattering everything.

'I seriously don't know where Mehak is and trust me, I was going to give my best performance today. I am afraid they either did something terrible or told Mahek everything,' Virat cried.

'How could you do such a stupid thing, Virat? What was running through your mind? You had practiced so hard and it was Mehak's dream to win. You just ruined everything. She was our friend,' Kavya said in a tone of dejection.

'Dammit! She was more than a friend to me. You know that. You know how much I loved her. Even I wanted her to win and…forget it. I know I am at fault here. I am really sorry.'

Virat kept his head on her shoulder and broke down in

tears. Breaking a girl's heart is way worse than we think it to be. It destroys everything—her future relationships, her ability to love and trust someone, and her inner peace and calm. Virat felt like he had broken Mahek's heart which was meant to beat for him. He called Mahek once again but got the same response. He wanted to throw his mobile away. He couldn't quite interpret what his feelings for Mahek meant. Sometimes they were friends, sometimes they behaved like they were more than friends, and now she was behaving like a complete stranger by not even telling him where she was.

Kavya was worried about Mehak and decided to go to her house and pay her a visit. She told Virat to go back home because she didn't want to create a scene at Mahek's place. Virat let her be because he didn't want to create another mess. Kavya assured him that she will meet him at his home after sorting things out with Mahek. The worst thing in life is not losing the one you love, it's losing yourself in the process of loving someone too much. Virat felt that he was addicted to Mahek and she was the only drug that could soothe his pain.

Virat reached home and as he entered the bedroom, he recollected the moments he had spent with Mehak. He opened his laptop and scrolled through their pictures that Kavya had taken of them while practicing their dance moves these past couple of days. Unable to bear her absence any longer, he shut down his laptop and was about to fall asleep when he saw a book on the table. It was Mahek's personal diary. She had forgotten it at his place during dance practice. Virat opened it and flipped through the pages to find his name sketched on one of the pages. He froze for a moment and his heart skipped a beat. What did it mean? Did she harbor feelings for him as well? He closed his eyes and wished for Mehak's happiness although he knew that he could no longer be the reason for her happiness anymore. He wasn't happy either, but he took out his mobile from his pocket and sent her a message:

I just saw the diary in which you had written my name. You left it for me intentionally, didn't you? Was it your way of letting me know about your feelings once we were done with our performance? This, in itself, shows that we are more than just friends. I know I hurt you but trust me, it was never planned. I used to pray for us to be alone, because I know we wouldn't ever run of things to say. We're both such freaks—we could've put silly acts up for days, but you left. You didn't even think about expressing your feelings? Not even once? You should have talked with me before disappearing into thin air. We could have sorted this out. I remember sitting next to you and occasionally trying to look into your eyes. It was different. The silence in that moment filled me with a warm happiness, like I had swallowed something too hot too fast. Mehak, can't you forgive me? Seriously, I feel like you're the password to my life. In your absence, I'm denied access to everything. I can neither drink nor eat.'

The message didn't reach her because her phone was switched off. He called Kavya up to ask how Mahek was doing.

'Is she at home?' Virat asked as soon as Kavya answered the call.

'Yes. She is at home but doesn't want to talk to you. She's just a bit upset,' Kavya said.

'Oh, thank God she's alright. What happened?'

'I will tell you everything once I reach your place. Don't take too much stress,' Kavya added.

Virat heaved a sigh of relief when he heard that Mehak was alright and nothing had happened to her. At the same time, he felt heartbroken when he realized that she was avoiding him on purpose. He tried to erase the last few hours from his memory and tried to get some sleep. It's said that you feel better when you don't think about what's bothering you, but when you care too much, everything reminds you of it. Every corner of his house reminded him of Mahek and he felt suffocated by it. The way she splashed water on him, the way they danced, the way they completed their assignments and so on. Sometimes, we play with love, but when you finally realize that you want to get serious, love plays with you.

Mehak's residence

'Do you know how many times we tried calling you? How can you be so irresponsible? It was all that you had been waiting for—your dream! And you gave it all up! For what?' Kavya bombarded Mahek with a million unanswered questions.

Kavya had come visiting without informing her and found her sitting on the bed, depressed and alone. Mehak sat with a dazed-like expression on her face, choosing to not answer any of Kavya's questions.

'Will you speak up, for god's sake?!' Kavya said raising her voice.

Mehak finally broke her silence.

'I didn't feel like participating today. I realized that winning a competition is worthless when you have lost something more important in life.'

'Will you jump straight to the point?' Kavya requested. She couldn't take the suspense anymore.

'Yes, I couldn't stop thinking about it last night. The fact that I wouldn't have ever found out whether I had won because of my talent and passion or because of Virat's false methods was reason enough for me to hold back.'

'What do you mean?' Kavya asked curiously.

'I had gone to college last night and I saw Virat in the corridor. I was about to call him but he went inside the auditorium. When I went towards the auditorium, I saw

Virat talking about something to the seniors. Then I listened carefully and saw him pleading to them, begging them to let us win because he wanted to win my love and could do anything for me. I left immediately and got back home weeping. I felt bad…I felt guilty. I felt cheated upon.'

'Do you know anything about what happened later?' Kavya asked.

Mehak told her that she had left soon after and didn't know what occurred next. Kavya conveyed to her everything that had happened so far and how badly Virat had been beaten by them. She even told her that Virat practiced their dance routine alone the entire night as this victory meant more to him than it did to her.

'He loves you. I've known him for ages and I have never seen him act like this before. He has transformed into a different and a better person since meeting you. He was just afraid of losing you because he knew how important winning the competition was to you. He didn't make any wrong deals with them and today if you both had won, it would have been because of your mere talent and nothing else. Why the hell would you back out? Why? Was it so easy for you, Mehak? We had dreamt of winning this together,' Kavya shouted.

'No, it wasn't easy. And I wasn't aware of the fact that they hurt Virat. I just didn't want to win the competition by sacrificing Virat's self-respect. I thought that winning that competition would inevitably make Virat look weak in front of those seniors; his self-respect was at stake. I can't see him lose his dignity in front of anyone just because of me. I know that he is very strong, mentally, but I felt like I'm the one who pressurized him and made it so hard for him. I constantly asked him whether we could perform to the best of our abilities or not. No Kavya, I didn't want to win by losing my way in life. His dignity and his self-respect mean much more to me than my dreams.'

Kavya was speechless and just stared at her without blinking.

'Do you mean....you...love...?' she stammered.

'Yes, I do. I've loved him ever since the very first day I met him!'

'Why did you never tell me about it?' Kavya asked in curiosity.

'Because earlier I thought that you two loved each other. You used to be together all the time and I thought that I might end up spoiling your relationship. So I never confessed my love for him. I realized it later when you and I became friends, and I planned on telling him everything today. But things didn't go as planned.'

'Everything will be fine. Just leave it to me.' Kavya had a big smile on her face and hugged her.

She left Mehak's home and called Virat, asking him to meet her at Aroma's. He requested her to tell him why, but Kavya didn't disclose anything and told him to reach there in the next couple of hours. Before leaving Mehak's place, Kavya had planned something with her, and had a surprise waiting for Virat who desperately wanted to know about Mehak. He had lost all hope, but he still loved her. Little did he know that even she loved him.

You can pick your friends, but you don't pick who you fall in love with. Such things are beyond control. Though Mehak had lost the competition, she was going to win her man's love. They both loved each other but had never expressed their feelings. Love is not about desire or wanting the person you love, it's about finding that person to be irresistibly desirable.

'Where are you, Kavya? I've been waiting here for an hour. Do you mind telling me what's going on?' Virat screamed.

Virat had been waiting for Kavya at Aroma's café since the past one hour but Kavya was ignoring him by disconnecting his calls and not replying to his messages. Finally, she called him up.

'I am not coming. Go back home. I will meet you later,' Kavya stated.

'What the fuck do you mean by that? Are you nuts?' Virat shouted.

Everyone in the café started staring at him. He disconnected the call and left the place. He tried to not think about Mehak too much; he tried to let go. But this was easier said than done. She was on his mind 24/7. Disheartened, he reached his apartment. He fished out the key from his pocket and unlocked the door. Little did he know that the shock of his life awaited him behind the door.

The lights had been dimmed and all the curtains shut. There were ribbons hanging from the walls and the room was filled with red and silver heart-shaped balloons. As he took a deep breath, Virat sniffed the aroma of scented candles that had been lit at different places in the room. Rose petals were scattered on the floor. Since it was still quite dark, it was difficult to make out if someone else was present in the room or not. His phone beeped and he read Kavya's text.

It's your day darling. This is what you've always wanted and here it is. Live the moment. I hope you like the arrangement and the decorations. I also hope that you will understand why I asked you to meet me at the coffee shop. That's the advantage of having a spare set of keys to your house. My party is due. I am not going to spare you. I will meet you tomorrow; today you should focus on your love life. Happy Valentine's Day. I know it's not Valentine's, but for you it might turn out to be one. Love you, my dumbo. Don't forget to kiss her. Lol. Bye.

Virat looked around to see if he could spot someone. There was a picture frame mounted on one of the walls. He moved closer to see the frame. It was a picture of Mehak with her arms around him, practicing one of their dance moves. They were looking into each other's eyes, as if deeply in love. There were a few more pictures of them that had been put up on the wall. Right next to the photo frame was a note.

One look at it and he knew it was Mahek's handwriting. *Life becomes romantic when our eyes start looking at someone silently, but it turns more romantic when that someone starts reading those eyes silently.*

Virat's heartbeats increased as he walked slowly towards his bedroom. He couldn't believe what he was witnessing. He felt as if he was watching a dream and someone would soon spill the water on him and wake him up. But it was all real. Just a few minutes back he had thought that he had lost his love forever, but here she was, waiting in the room for him. Virat opened the door and saw that even the bedroom had been decorated in a similar manner. There were candles and red-silver balloons everywhere. As he opened the door, a song started playing.

Sathiya…yeh tune kya kiya…Beliya ye tune kya kiya…

Maine kiya tera intazar…Maine kiya hai tumse pyaar.

And there she was—standing beside the stereo in her little blue dress. Mahek looked at him and smiled a shy smile as he entered the room. Virat was spellbound and his eyes popped out the way they do in comic films. Mahek looked ravishing—the dress clung to her like second skin and her hair blew softly in the air. Her eyes looked like the epitome of innocence and as she looked at him, he could not help but fall in love with her all over again. Her sensual, glossy lips glittered like stars in the night sky. Before Virat could say anything, she spoke in her mesmerizing voice,

'Can I have a dance with you?' Virat was left gaping at her. There was no way he was going to deny himself this opportunity. He took her hand in his and swirled her around.

Itni mohabbat seh na sakunga, sach maano zinda reh na sakunga,
Tujhko sambhaalu, ye mera jimma, mai hu toh kya hai jaane tamanna…
Ab jina marna mera, jaanam tere haath hai.
Toh phir sambhal…le me chalaa…
Jana kaha…aa dil me aa!

Hand in hand, their feet moved in rhythm to the music as he held her firmly by her waist. They were standing so close to each other that they could inhale each other's breath. They kept dancing for the next few minutes without speaking a word.

'Virat, I want to tell you something,' said Mahek finally breaking the silence.

'Yeah?'

'Are you sure?'

'About what?' He knew the much awaited moment had arrived finally.

Mahek came closer and whispered something in his ear.

'Virat…I wanted to tell you that…I…I love… I love how we can just look at each other and smile.'

'That's it?' Virat asked.

'And…I love you.'

Virat kissed both her eyes and gently tucked behind her ear the lose strand of hair that fell on her forehead. He finally spoke, 'When I met you, I found you were an absolute sweetheart. But you are more than that. When I first started talking to you, I found you were a darling. But you are more than that. When I started to discuss my problems with you, I found you were super cute. But you are more than that. Everything that I had assumed about you was wrong, but one thing was right…you are my sweet baby and I love you for exactly who you are. Your presence has added value to my life and I hope it continues like this forever. I love you too.'

It was a special day for both of them. It was one of those moments that get etched in your memory for a lifetime. The looked into each other's eyes for one more time before their lips met. His arms enveloped her into a hug. If anything could make her feel safe, it was a hug from him. She broke the kiss as quickly as it began. He leaned forward, again, as though he was seeking her approval and this time she too leaned closer and kissed him passionately. Everything else seemed inconsequential in that moment. It was a moment they would treasure all their lives. That kiss was to be the start of a beautiful relationship.

Were We Never Meant to Be?

Relationships are strange and undefinable. No matter what name you give them, it all comes down to one thing: trust. But the funny thing is, even if you trust each other the most, if you're not meant to be together, you won't be. Even though Virat and Mehak had been going to the same college for over a year, they never noticed each other before, though their paths met time and again. Look at them now—together, in a relationship, in love.

Many a times we know in our hearts what's true and what's not. But for some people, when the truth is finally spoken, it brings happiness into their lives, and for some it is hard to digest the truth. When Mehak told Virat that she loved him, he was beyond delighted. But on the other hand, when Zoya spoke the truth, it completely shattered Rohan.

'You know that you won't ever be happy with the decision you're making, so why are you doing this to yourself?' asked Rohan trying to convince Zoya but nothing worked.

Zoya had called him to meet her one last time before they parted ways. The time they had spent together had been one of the most fulfilling experiences of her life and she wanted to end things on a good note. She respected him and didn't want to see him get hurt.

'Rohan, please understand that we can't be together. Just always remember that someone somewhere is happy knowing that you are happy. Plus, there is someone better waiting for you out there. Someone who will give you more love than I could ever. So always smile and I will pray to God that you may achieve all your dreams,' Zoya said, holding his hand firmly.

'How can I be happy without you? I love you,' he cried.

'You have to be. If you want me to be happy, then you have to do this for me.'

Rohan didn't show any reaction and kept looking at her. Zoya was feeling equally bad, but she had no other option left. She had to sacrifice her happiness, else it would destroy his. She kissed him on his cheeks for the last time and somehow managed to make him smile.

'Promise me something,' she said.

Rohan looked at her with a quizzical expression.

'Promise me, you will never keep anything hidden from me—like when you find another girl to love.'

'Shut up,' he said in annoyance. 'I don't think I'm capable of loving anyone else but you.'

'Ok, should I look for someone for you instead? What

kind of a girl do you like?'

'Like you don't know.'

'Listen, find a girlfriend who loves you, and don't just go by her appearance. Looks will die with time. She should be able to take care of you in your hard times and understand your needs. Got it?'

She tried hard to get his mind off the breakup, but the fact was, whatever she said made perfect sense. Though Rohan's logical mind knew it, his heart was not willing to accept the truth. They hugged for the last time, smiled, and parted ways. There are some things we don't want to acknowledge but we have to accept them anyway. There are people who we can't live without but we have to sometimes let them go.

People say actions speak louder than words, but sometimes it's the words that hurt the most. Actions are easy to ignore, but words hit you right where it hurts. Zoya's words had disturbed Rohan completely and the feeling of hopelessness engulfed him. As each day passed, he turned into more of a loner and avoided sharing his feelings with anyone. It was only Riddhima who consoled him and stood by him in those bad times. Keeping her own feelings for him aside, she helped him recover from the breakup. Sometimes, he shared his agony with me too.

'Why is it that the people you care about the most end

up making you feel so meaningless?' Rohan asked me during one of our midnight chat sessions on the phone.

'Rohan, get over it. There's no point living in the past. Zoya is your past now. You need to understand she can't be in your life anymore. Instead of remembering the pain she gave you, you should be happy with all the memories you built with her,' I said trying to make him understand.

'I know, Adi. I agree with you. But sometimes it feels like I don't deserve true love in my life. I don't deserve happiness like the rest. Why do bad things have to happen to me every time? Why?'

'Love is never wrong. But your choice can be. Rohan, you have to just open your heart to someone who deserves it.'

Saying so, I hung up the phone. I knew that the hardest thing ever is to accept that the one you chose to love couldn't love you back enough. It gets all the more difficult when you have to move on in life without the person you always thought would walk beside you. Rohan re-read all the messages that Zoya had sent him. He had saved some special ones in a folder and tried to delete them in a fit of anger.

He sent her a message again:

I miss you terribly. Why did you choose to walk away from me? Every bit of you is ingrained in me. The sound of your voice awakens my soul. I could sit here and write about what I love about you all day and I still wouldn't cover it all. I still feel that we are together. You haven't left my thoughts. Never.

Not even once. To put it quite simply, I miss you. I miss the way you would confide in me. I miss the stories you would tell me. I miss your smile. I miss every moment spent with you. I despise every moment without you. I could spend hours trying to explain why it still hurts, but all I wanna tell you is that I miss you. However, I have no clue whether you do or you don't. I would have fought for you but you never acted like it would be worth the fight.

As always, Zoya didn't reply. When you spend so much time with another person, you get so used to their presence around you that their absence hurts you. Even your likes and dislikes change accordingly. It's completely normal to miss those moments once that person chooses to walk away from you. Your heart will be broken, stomped on, crushed and shattered, until you find that one person who can put it all back together again.

We never really get over the person we once loved; we just learn to keep going on with our lives, resigned to our fate. As time passed, Rohan too learned to deal with his past, but sometimes the memories of Zoya still haunted him. With time, he understood his priorities and decided to concentrate on what lied ahead of him rather than what he had left behind. He wanted to build his life all over again. He tried to keep himself busy as much as possible, not because he wanted to achieve something big, but because he wanted a reason to forget his past memories. Riddhima acted as a solvent to it and her presence in his life comforted him. With her silly jokes and comforting nature, she was able to make him smile.

'Rohan, why are you crying? I told you that I can't see tears in your eyes,' Riddhima said as Rohan came out of the kitchen.

Since Rohan had an off on weekends, he would visit Riddhima's house to help her with the daily chores.

'I am not crying, this onion…' Rohan said wiped his tears away.

'What are you doing with that onion? Just leave it and come here,' Riddhima said while cleaning the showcase.

'This onion is after my life; it's making me cry.'

'By the way, in this get-up, you look like the ideal maid,' Riddhima teased pointing at the kitchen apron he had donned over his outfit with a glint of mischief in her eyes.

'You jerk, I will kill you. Do I look like a maid to you? Please, maids are not as sexy as me.'

'They are. I can show you a few of them if you want me to.'

Riddhima pinched him on his arm and ran away. Rohan ran after her, throwing cushions at her to obstruct her path. He grabbed her just in time and pinned her down on the sofa. They both looked at each other and started giggling.

'I am so happy to see you smiling again. I thought that I'd lose you and that smile of yours, considering the way you have been acting since your breakup,' Riddhima uttered.

'Rohan's smile disappeared as he heard the word 'breakup'.

After a few seconds of silence, Riddhima went into the kitchen in order to make coffee for him to better his mood. Rohan sat thinking about how his life had changed in the last couple of months. Sometimes, a cup of coffee and a good friend make life much better. It's never easy to act as a friend around the person who you love and wish to spend the rest of your life with. Riddhima loved him, yet she acted like a friend and did whatever it took to make him happy.

Dreaming of You

22nd December, 2009

It's a myth that people and relationships don't change. In fact, both keep evolving with the passage of time. As time passes us by, we go through so much that we grow into a different person altogether and thus the nature of our relationship changes. In the past few months, Rohan had witnessed things that he had never experienced before in his life. Some people told him not to let go of what he couldn't live without, but actually it was holding on to that thing that was tearing him apart. He had understood and accepted that Zoya couldn't be part of his life anymore. He deleted all her messages and didn't keep any contact with her. Neither did she. Time and again, her words would reverberate in his ears: *Someone, somewhere is happy knowing that you are happy.* He didn't hate her, but he had lost all the reasons to love her. Sometimes you love, learn, and then move on, which is perfectly fine as not everything is meant to last forever.

Post their break-up, he had begun to spend more and more time with Riddhima. She was his pillar of strength who helped him move on and he loved being with her. However, she was still just a friend and his French teacher, nothing more. Every minute you spend with someone you aren't meant to be with, takes away the time you could have instead spent with the right person you should have been with in the first place. For her, Rohan was that right person. He too had slowly developed feelings for her but was afraid of taking things to the next level.

Virat supported Rohan post his break-up, explaining to him why it was important to move on in life and not pay heed to what had happened. His funda in life was 'let bygones be bygones'. He tried to make Rohan see what a wonderful girl Riddhima was. He firmly believed that Rohan won't ever find another girl like her, someone who stood by him, selflessly, during his ups and downs even when he was in a relationship with Zoya. He told him to take a chance with Riddhima and figure out if she was really the one for him. He didn't want Rohan to regret not having tried his luck with her.

'Where are you? I'm waiting near the canteen,' Kavya told Virat over the phone.

'I am at the gate. See you in 5 minutes.'

Even though Virat was now dating Mahek, nothing changed between Kavya and him. They still were the best of friends who would do stupid things together, be it teasing, irritating, or insulting each other. The fact is you're not really best friends until you start insulting each other on a daily basis. Virat was someone who would do anything for a good friend and Kavya was on top of that friend list. Whenever she was in a fix, Virat would come to her rescue, leaving everything behind.

After he parked his car, Virat sent a text message to Mehak as he walked towards the canteen.

Waiting for you in the canteen. Come soon. I want to feel you touch. Love you. Muaah.

Mehak's reply soon followed:

I want to feel not only your touch but much more. Waiting to see you. Love you more.

A girl can be your best friend, your lover, your worst enemy, or your worst nightmare. It all depends on how you treat her. Virat pampered both the girls who were special to him in their own, unique way. Mahek never tried to keep Virat away from Kavya; she never felt insecure. She had full faith in Virat and their love which grew stronger with each passing day. She had kept her relationship a secret from her family because she didn't want any unnecessary complications. Involving the family would mean having restrictions on going out late with her friends and she didn't want to lose that freedom. Moreover, her family was the conservative kind and wouldn't have accepted Virat so easily knowing that he had lost his parents early on in life and didn't have a career yet.

'Where is Mahek?' Kavya asked as soon as Virat reached the canteen.

'She must be reaching anytime now. I have informed her that we are here.'

'Let's order something while we wait for her. I'm famished.'

As Virat was ordering something at the counter, Mehak surprised him from behind by hugging him. For a few seconds they forgot that they were in canteen and not in their bedroom, but it hardly bothered them. Virat turned and pecked her on the cheek. He ordered Misal-Pav for her as it was her favourite dish. Back at the table, all three of them gossiped about how bad their college was and how their professors acted like psychos. No matter how reputed our colleges are, we love to curse it and even if it has the best teaching staff, we love to abuse our professors.

'You should see our Organizational Behaviour professor peep into the classroom when he notices a female professor teaching. His speed slows down automatically, and he scans them from top to bottom,' Kavya said.

'We should make his MMS too. What say?' Mehak added.

'Oh please, I don't want to get thrown out of college,' Virat said sarcastically.

'Anyway, we never actually attend classes, do we? We just eat at here at the canteen or roam about in the campus,' Kavya laughed and everyone joined in.

While they were talking, Virat felt a hand lingering on his inner thighs, under the table. He froze for a moment and looked around to scan the room and see if anyone was noticing them.

'Ouch!' Virat screamed.

'What happened to you? Why did you scream?' Kavya asked, unaware of what was happening.

'Nothing. I am absolutely fine.'

Mehak laughed and continued to pinch his thighs. Virat reciprocated by grazing the sole of his feet against her thigh.

They continued teasing each other like this for some time until Mahek sent him a message.

I want to be alone with you. Let's go to some classroom.

Virat replied saying,

'What if someone enters the classroom? We will be fucked.'

Mehak gave him an irritated look and replied:

You always act dumb. We will ask Kavya to stand outside the classroom and keep a watch.

Virat looked at her in a state of shock. But the more he thought about it, the more exciting the idea seemed. After all, Kavya was their friend who knew everything about them. And they didn't have to disclose everything to her. They could simply say they needed the privacy of the classroom to discuss something important. Looking at her seductive eyes, he felt a sudden urge to devour her against the hard, cold wall of the classroom. He asked both girls to follow him.

'Where to?' Kavya questioned.

'I'll tell you. Let's leave from here first.'

Kavya and Mehak followed Virat as he left the canteen. Virat turned and looked at Mahek who was still smiling. Kavya again asked where they were going in curiosity.

'Kavya, there's something important we wanna discuss and we need your help in that,' Virat hushed.

Mahek was walking behind them and couldn't stop her laughter, but whenever Kavya turned, she changed her expression to one of seriousness.

'Actually, Mehak and I had a big fight yesterday and want to sort things out. So we want to be left alone in some classroom for some time to talk things out...'

Before he could continue, Kavya interrupted him,

'Why alone in the classroom?'

'Where else should we go? Should we create a scene in

front of everyone? You know very well that a girl in a bad mood is the most dangerous creature on this planet. So I need some protection,' Virat added.

When he further told her that she had to wait outside and keep a check, Kavya almost killed Virat.

'Now, you want me to be your security guard? So mean. Mehak, look, your boyfriend is really mean. Let's look for someone better for you. Someone really hot and not mean like him.'

'What the fuck, you…' he shouted but paused realizing that an argument with Kavya would prolong the act.

Eventually, Kavya agreed and they entered an empty first-floor classroom. Virat promised Kavya that he would buy her a drink or two for helping them out. Kavya hit him hard on his back and gave him an angry look. Virat gave her a flying kiss and told her to lock the door from outside so no passersby could suspect anything. Kavya stood outside the door in the passage pretending that she was waiting for someone.

'More than anything else, I am afraid of Kavya opening the door,' Virat said as he pulled Mahek closer.

Mahek smiled and pulled his cheeks lovingly. Virat pushed her against the wall and leaned in to give her a kiss She shyly turned her face away. Virat proceeded to kiss her neck, then her ears, then eyes. She felt a wild sensation running through her body. Getting intimate in a public place further added to the pleasure. They were nervous but equally thrilled, afraid that they'd hear a knock. Virat rolled his fingers inside her t-shirt and kissed her passionately. She returned his kisses with equal fervor.

Once done cuddling, they sat on the bench and Mahek opened her lunch box. She had cooked green pea rice along with some yoghurt especially for Virat. In fact, one of the reasons why she wanted to be alone with him was to make him eat with her own hands. When your heart starts to function, your brain begins to malfunction.

'Why do you love me so much?' Virat asked.

'I don't know, but I can't live without you. I feel safe with you,' Mehak replied, feeding him the rice.

'I am so lucky to have you. You're not my life, you're the one I want to spend it with. You're not my world, you're the best thing in it,' Virat added.

Once done eating the lunch, he gave her a peck on the cheek as a 'thank you' gesture.

'That's it? That's all I get for cooking you such yummy food?' The spark in Mahek's eyes and her seductive looks made him horny. He grabbed her by the waist and made her lie down on the bench. He saw the nervousness in her eyes and kissed her forehead.

'I just want to look at every inch of your body,' Virat said as he stood up.

He couldn't control himself anymore and pounced on her like a wild beast. He started kissing her wildly, like there was no tomorrow. Lost in the ecstasy of passionate love, he bit her slightly hard on the neck and she screamed loudly in response. Virat looked at her for a second and gave her a small peck where he bit her. Mahek wrapped her hands around him and kissed his neck. As Virat's hands tried to explore her body, pulling her top up, they heard their door being opened. They immediately got up and tried to pretend like nothing had happened, but to their dismay, Kavya had seen more than she had bargained for. She broke into laughter looking at them.

Virat looked at her, embarrassed, while Mahek was still pulling down her t-shirt.

'Fuck, this is hilarious. I should have hung the "Do not disturb" sign outside,' she laughed till the point her stomach pained.

'Kavya, you should have knocked first. Shit man, you made my heart jump,' said Virat almost getting a heart attack.

'You think I didn't know what you guys were doing inside? You both are dumb . The moment you started texting each other in the canteen, I knew that you wanted to board a railgaadi.'

'What railgaadi?' Mahek asked with a puzzled look.

'Sex, foreplay…whatever you'd like to call it,' she winked.

Mahek turned red in embarrassment. Kavya screamed when Virat pulled her ears as if he was punishing a kid. Virat felt like a batsman who is run out, and right when he thinks his time is up, the umpire declares it a 'no ball', much to the relief of the batsman. Kavya told them that she didn't open the door for fun but because she saw the head of their department on his daily rounds. All of them immediately left the classroom. As they walked out, they glanced at each other and burst into laughter at what had just happened. There is no feeling more comforting and consoling than knowing that you are in the company of the one you love. Rare are such relationships where you hold no grudges, no complaints, and no insecurities.

'How about going to your place for some fun rather than going for a movie?' Mahek asked.

Virat had dropped Kavya home and was heading for a movie with Mehak. While on their way to the movie hall, Mehak suggested they go his place instead. As soon as Mehak mentioned going to his home for fun, a picture of a chemist shop flashed in his mind. He immediately turned his car around and gave a wicked smile to Mahek. He stopped the car near a chemist shop he had never been to before. He did this deliberately so he won't feel awkward while asking for a condom. Another reason why he preferred going to an unknown chemist was that he had never purchased a condom before in his life. It was his first time and he felt uneasy asking for it at the counter. He couldn't express his uneasiness to Mahek because she would've made fun of him, hurting his male ego. Though he was aware of the brands and the flavours because of the advertisements, when his time came, he didn't know which one to order. *Maybe I should have asked Mahek*, he thought. *After all, she is the one who will have to...* Brushing aside his thoughts, he mustered courage and walked towards the counter. There were a couple of customers at the counter and he waited till the salesperson cleared their bills.

'Yes, what do you want?' one of the guys at the counter asked Virat.

'You can clear their bills first. I'm in no hurry. I'll just speak with my friend till then,' he said pretending to call someone.

He looked out the glass door and saw Mahek looking back at him in anticipation. He signalled saying he'd be back in 2 minutes, pretending to be on a call with someone. The truth was, he had called customer care instead, as he was fucking nervous to take a step forward. He had never felt such tension before, not even during his exams. Now he understood why people called 'love-making' an art.

'Son, what do you need?' the counter guy asked Virat once again.

'I need...give me one...Crocin and D-cold,' Virat said feeling the tension build up in his body. *Shit, man. Come on Virat, you can do it. You have to do it. You are a man,* he told himself.

Suddenly, the person standing next to him asked for a *Moods* condom packet.

'Give me one, too. Also, add a 5-star to my bill. How much, uncle?'

Just to cover up for the condoms, he had asked for a 5-star chocolate as well. The guy at the counter understood the reason behind Virat's uneasiness and gave him a comforting smile. Finally, the first battle had been won! Virat left the counter after paying the bill. He opened the door to the car and gave Mahek a wide smile. Making love is not just about sex, it's a battle of hormones that starts from asking a condom at the chemist shop.

'Got it?' Mahek asked.

'Yeah, It was easy. I was just receiving an important call so it took some time. Take this—this is for you, my darling,' Virat proudly declared, giving her both the condom and the 5-star he had bought to save him some humiliation.

She gave him a kiss on the cheek and they left for his home. Virat parked the car, lifted her up in his arms, and carried her inside the house

As soon as Virat closed the door, Mehak embraced him lovingly. She buried her face in his shoulder while he wrapped an arm around her, returning the hug. He pulled her back to him as she tried to escape and smooched her hungrily. She finally pulled away from him and ran towards the kitchen. He ran after her, wrapping his arms around her waist and lifting her up in the air. When he placed her back on the ground, she turned to look at him amusingly.

'Go take a shower first,' she teased and escaped from his

grip, leaving Virat disappointed. He went to freshen up and asked her to make herself comfortable.

While Virat took a bath, Mahek removed a note from her bag, knowing that Virat would head straight for his wardrobe once he was out of the bathroom. She kept the note on top of his clothes and quickly changed into her shorts without taking her heels off. Virat got out of the shower with nothing but a towel wrapped around his waist. His bare body looked very seductive, with water dripping all over his chest. She gazed at him in admiration. Virat was about to pick up tee from the wardrobe when he saw the note. He picked the note up. It said,

Fill in the blanks:

I'm lusting for your ____. I want you to lick my ____ and ____ over and over again. I even want to feel your ____ in my ____.

Virat looked at Mahek and said, 'So this was all your planning, eh?'

Mahek bit her lip seductively and said, 'Are you just going to stand there lusting for me or are you going to do something about it?'

She was speaking in such a sexy tone that he couldn't resist pouncing on her. She let out a moan and in a few seconds, he grabbed her and pushed her on the bed. She licked his fingers one by one and then traced the outline of his lips. It made his body tingle.

'If you could picture what's going through my mind right now, you'd be totally, and I mean *totally*, turned on,' he whispered in her ears.

'What's that?' she asked while encircling his nipples with her fingernails.

The room had been dimly lit, creating a passionate ambience for lovemaking. Virat removed the deck of cards from the drawer.

'Let's play a game,' Virat declared. 'These are a pack of playing cards. We assign a sexual act to each suit symbol like kisses for diamonds, body rub for spades, rolling of fingers for heart, and trying out a new position for clubs. Each number represents the wildness of the act. The higher the number, the wilder you'll have to be.'

'I am up for it,' Mahek responded.

She picked the first card up and it was an 8 of diamonds which meant kisses. The next moment, she leaned over him and started kissing him all over his body. From neck till toe, she kissed him 7 times, and gave him a final passionate kiss on his lips. Virat picked the next card and it was a 10 of hearts. He slowly undressed her, first removing her shorts and then the t-shirt. She still had her heels on and Virat was about to remove that too, but she told him not to.

'I want to make out wearing just my heels. Doesn't it turn you on?' she asked.

Virat nodded and slowly started rolling his fingers all over her, starting from her neck onwards. He paused near her belly and kissed it, making her moan loudly. The game continued for some time till Mehak grabbed the hem of his boxers and pulled down. She rolled her necklace on his body in such a manner that it aroused his senses. She stopped rolling near his inner thighs and looked above. Virat's eyes were shut.

'Look at me while you make love to me. Look here Virat. Look me in the eyes,' she moaned.

He gave her a sexy smile as he came up and hugged her. It was all happening too quickly. Virat took charge and Mehak screamed loudly. She wrapped her legs around his waist and Virat penetrated her slowly.

'Virat,' she whispered stroking his hair. 'You put something in the food. Didn't you?' she said with a satisfaction on her face.

'Hmm,' he giggled.

'And Virat…'

'Hmm?'

'This was indeed amazing,' she panted, curling up on his sweaty chest.

Mehak kissed him. Virat responded with the same excitement and they hugged each other.

'You know what?' Virat said as he stroked her hair.

Mehak looked into his eyes and slowly kissed his cheeks like a small baby.

'Shit, we forgot to use the condom,' Virat said, remembering the lengths he had gone to buy them.

'It's ok. We are safe. You pulled out at the right time,' she replied.

'It's not about safety. It was about my effort. Leave it, you will never understand,' Virat said sadly.

Only he knew what all he had done to get that *Moods* packet but in the end everything happened so quickly that Mahek was not in a mood to even wait for a second. Neither was Virat. Virat played their song on his mobile and hugged her,

Dil ke chaman ka hasna toh dekho,
Jaage nazar ka sapna toh dekho.
Aise hue hum, ek jaan ek dil,
Tu hai ki me hu, kehna hai mushkil…
Zhoka basanti hai tu…tan hai gulaabi mera!!
Do rang milne ke baad, hote nahi hai judaa…
Saathiya tune kya kiya…itna karo na mujhe pyaar!!

Virat and Mehak were lost in each other's arms, with not a care in the world.

The next morning, Mehak woke up content in Virat's arms. She saw the time and woke up Virat as it was getting late. They got ready and Virat decided to drop Mahek home. Before leaving the house, they kissed each other one more

time before locking the door. Virat took his bike instead of the car to avoid the morning traffic. He dropped her outside her home in Aundh. On his way back, he saw Rohan smoking near a paanwala. He immediately stopped his bike and greeted him. He was delighted to see him and puzzled as well

'How come you are here in Aundh?' Virat asked.

'I had come to meet my aunt who stays here. I was just on my way back home. What about you?'

'Pick and drop service for my girlfriend, you see,' Virat winked.

Rohan laughed and offered a cigarette to Virat. Virat helped himself to one ciggie and asked him whether he had moved on. Rohan nodded affirmatively. He confessed that he was confused about certain decisions in life and wanted to discuss them with Virat at length just to ease his stress.

'Can we meet on Sunday?' Rohan asked, looking at the calendar on his mobile phone.

'Yes. Why not? Anything serious?'

'Kind of. Even my brother Aditya would like to join us, if that's okay with you,' Rohan said.

'C'mon buddy, I am completely okay with it.'

They bid goodbye to each other and went their separate ways.

We often meet people unintentionally in our lives without knowing that they would become our well-wishers some day. Rohan never thought that he would share his worries with someone he had met only a couple of times. Plus he never expected Virat to support and guide him through the rough patches in his life.

It's not about how long you've know each other or how often you meet. If your wavelength matches, then one meeting is all it takes.

Yes, I Cared...

26th December, 2009, Sunday

It was a chilly winter morning in Pune. The morning breeze waited to bring a new dawn in Rohan's life. We had decided to meet Virat at the Germany Bakery in Koregaon Park. Since it was a Sunday, the place was jam packed. It was quite a popular joint and probably one of the oldest ones too. We had ordered a ginger lemon tea and a non-veg club sandwich to begin with, as Rohan anticipated it was going to be a long discussion.

'Guys, I understand that you are saying this for my betterment, but I am afraid of getting into a relationship again. If someone hurts you, it's difficult to recover from the trauma, no matter how hard you try. The experience makes you cynical about love itself,' Rohan sobbed.

'Rohan, don't be so stubborn. Everyone has a past, but not everyone keeps on crying about it. If you keep on going like this, you will never find happiness in your life. And why are you being so selfish thinking just about yourself? Think about Riddhima who did so much for you when you needed a helping hand. Don't lose out on such a girl. You'll regret it later on,' Virat added.

'You are complicating things for no reason. If someone can't be with you due to some reason, that's okay. Some come back and some don't. It's part and parcel of life. And just because one person leaves, it doesn't mean that you should forget about everyone else who's still standing by your side. It's really commendable that Riddhima supported you as your best friend even though she loved you. Just think how life would have been without her,' I said trying to convince him to accept Riddhima's love and move on.

Rohan was about to say something when the waiter arrived with the sandwich and the ginger lemon tea. It was one of the best sandwiches I had ever tasted.

Rohan took a sip of the tea and continued, 'I am not denying that Riddhima was the one who was my backbone during my hard times, but the only thing that scares me is that there shouldn't be any complications again. She is a couple of years older than me.'

'Don't act like a fool. I know your parents really well and I am sure they will be absolutely fine with it. Otherwise I would have warned you long back. Why didn't you think of all this when you were in a relationship with Zoya? Weren't the complications more then? Also, you've told me her parents are super cool. So why are you worrying so much? Just don't think so much about it and go ahead. You have my support, bro,' I said taking a bite of my sandwich.

'Absolutely. Just move on,' Virat agreed.

'Aditya and Virat, you must be thinking I'm emotionless and that's why I ignore Riddhima's love, but it's not that. I never treated her badly. I always respected her love and even shared my feelings with her. You might think that if I decide to move on, it would mean that I never loved Zoya in the first place, but that's not true. I really loved her and was ready to fight for my love, but she had her own priorities. I respected her love too. I remember she had asked me to love someone who loved me back and took care of me. I think Riddhima is the right person. But don't ever think that I didn't love Zoya,' Rohan confessed with tears in his eyes.

'Have you lost it? We all know how much you loved Zoya and how hard you tried to convince her not to leave. I always asked you to move on, but never forced you as I wanted you to be ready for it. It's easy to fall for someone when you are lonely. But then, that's nothing but an escape from your previous relationship. Trust me Rohan, true love is always better than first love. I am saying this from personal experience,' Virat responded.

Virat and I finally sweet-talked him into giving it a try and he finally caved in. Just to celebrate his new innings, we ordered a carrot cake which was just perfect for the occasion. After some time, we decided to leave as Virat had some personal work to attend to. I didn't prod too much since Rohan had once told me Virat preferred keeping his personal life peronal.

'Give me the good news soon,' Virat said and left.

We also went back home with a new hope in our mind. A hope that would erase all the bad memories of the past and rewrite the good ones to bring the smile back into Rohan's life. He knew what it took to love someone. One should not ask a person who's in love to define love; instead they should ask the one who has lost someone in the name of love. Rohan had lost the love of his life once, and was ready to start things all over with Riddhima.

Kitaabon ke pannon ko palat ke sochta hun,
Yun palat jaaye meri zindagi to kya baat hai.
Hawa ke zhoke ko jab jab dekhta hu tab sochta hu,
Aisi hi aage bad jaaye zindagi toh kya baat hai.

Kalam toh thi hi haath me par likhna sikhaaya hai aapne,
Taakat toh thi hi haath me par hosla dilaya hai aapne.
Manzil toh thi hi saamne par raasta dikhaaya hai aapne,
Hum toh sirf dost hi the, par aashiq banaya hai aapne!

Have you ever fallen for a close friend and been unsure as to what you should do about it? Rohan had fallen in love with Riddhima, slowly but surely. The way she handled him and never turned her back to his problems made him feel special. But he wasn't sure whether he should really take it forward or wait for the right time. But, as they say, there is never a time or a place for true love. It happens by chance, in a heartbeat, in a single throbbing moment.

He was confused because he had never felt like that for her before, or maybe he had overlooked his feelings for her. So what hurts the most? Saying something and wishing you hadn't, or not saying something and wishing you had? Rohan was in a dilemma and thought of talking to Zoya once before taking any step further.

This time he wanted to have a word with her not to plead or beg for his love, but to tell her that he had found someone worth his love. Life is not about finding someone you can live with. It's more about finding that someone who can't live without you. He hadn't called her once in the last few months and thus he felt a little weird calling her again. He dialled her number anxiously. As soon as he heard the ringtone, he immediately disconnected the call. He gathered the courage and again dialled her number.

'The number you have dialled is busy on another call,' came the automated response.

He decided to send her a message instead, but just when he was typing out the message, his phone beeped with a call. The name on the screen sent shivers down his spine. It was Zoya.

'Hello,' Rohan said in a shaky voice.

'Hello. I got a call from you.'

'Yes. How are you?' Rohan stammered.

'I am fine. But who is this? Do I know you? Sorry, but your number is not saved,' Zoya said in a casual tone.

'Rohan.'

'Rohan…who?' she said as if she had never heard the name before in her life.

Her statement came as a shock to Rohan and he got extremely angry.

'How many Rohans have been a part of your life till date, Zoya? You've forgotten my voice too? I wonder if you ever loved me,' he screamed loudly.

'Why have you called me, Rohan? I have moved on and I'm trying to live my life without you,' she said in a soft tone.

'Yes, I called you for the same reason. I am moving on. Better late than never.'

'Good luck, Rohan.'

Before Rohan could say anything, she disconnected the call. It made him more furious and he immediately sent her a couple of long messages:

Till this minute, I was confused whether I was taking the right step, but now I am no more in a dilemma. Now I understand that everything happens for a reason. I don't know what got into me that I called you. You asked me who I was… You are right. Who am I? I never meant anything to you. Tell me—if

I meant anything to you, how you could forget the sound of my voice? This completely baffles me. Suddenly, I can see everything that I had been ignoring for the last few months. You have no place for me in your heart. You have no respect for me, not in the tiniest bit. If you did, then you would not treat me the way you do. You would not string me along and play with my emotions. I fight with myself over and over again because I feel like such a loser for staying in a relationship that made me so unhappy. I wonder why I clung to your memories when everyone and told me to let go. How can I defend you? I'm always sticking up for you when my friends ask me the reason for our breakup. I tell them you were nice but just that situation was beyond your control.

Don't expect me to wish you a happy birthday every year, like I have since I met you. If you recall, the first day I met you was actually on your birthday. Don't expect me to be there when you need me. I will never again run my fingers through your hair or cuddle up next to you. Don't look forward to anything from me anymore. And please understand that I am not doing this to teach you a lesson. I am doing this because I am finally done with you. I am just fed up, and my heart can't take it anymore. I have finally made peace with the fact that we can never be together again.

There's always a right time to end everything. If Rohan had not called Zoya, he would have never found the courage to start a new relationship. But now he had made up his mind. He had decided to move on and he had the right to be happy. Every person who comes into your life teaches you something, plays his part and departs. No one lives with you forever. You never lose anyone because you never owned them in the first place. Rohan didn't lose anything but he would have certainly lost an opportunity to be with a person who loved him like anything if he wouldn't have taken the decision to be happy.

As he lay on his bed, he remembered the day he was with Riddhima after ending the usual class of French at her home...

Rohan was ill and on medication. Still he had gone for the classes, not because he was passionate about French but because he loved Riddhima's company. That day Riddhima had invited him for dinner. After having their dinner, Rohan had intentionally pretended that he had forgotten his tablets home and would take them once he gets back. But Riddhima had forcefully grabbed his bag from him and digged through the contents. She had found the tablets wrapped in a piece of paper and told Rohan to take them. Rohan hated medicines and always put up an act to avoid eating them. Riddhima knew he would've hidden the bag somewhere and hence brought a glass of water and sat beside him.

'Come on, eat. Stop being so dramatic.'

'Why should I listen to you? You are not my mom,' Rohan muttered.

'Whatever. Take this and put it in your mouth.'

Rohan took one tablet in his hand but was not ready to eat it. Riddhima somehow convinced him and forced him to insert the tablet in his mouth. Riddhima gave him the glass of water but he showed slight resistance.

'Are you taking it or should I stop talking to you forever?' Riddhima said trying to emotionally blackmail him.

'Why do you have to say such things? I hate it,' Rohan said giving her an angry look.

'Then without overacting, just drink the water and finish it,' Riddhima said going closer to him.

'Please, I am sorry. I will take my medicines tomorrow onwards,' Rohan pleaded.

Whenever it came to medication, be it taking tablets or visiting a doctor, he always tried to find an escape route. But Riddhima never allowed him and always forced him as he was very careless when it came to his health.

'Are you eating or should I leave?' she shouted.

As Rohan drank the water, he looked at Riddhima from the corner of his eye and smirked. Riddhima told him to open his mouth wide open and rechecked if he had hidden the tablet. After making sure he hadn't, she pulled his cheeks and gave him a wide smile.

Rohan recollected many such sweet moments when Riddhima had expressed her care and love for him and how he always chose to overlook them. Thinking about them, he felt the same love for her and realized what he was losing out on. He lied down on the bed, excited to start his new life.

If someone in our lives makes us forget the haunting memories of our past, then that someone is surely a part of our future. Riddhima not only helped him get over his depression, she also gave him hope for the future. He thought about expressing his love in a special way so that he could capture the moment forever. He came up with different ideas to make it memorable for her as it was his turn to make Riddhima feel loved.

He thought of messaging Riddhima how much he was missing her, remembering their days together. But when it came down to writing the message, he found that he was at a loss for words, though he didn't need words because he had found an amazing person who could understand his silence. After a long time, he had a smile on his face.

Unofficially Yours

27th December, 2009

'Adi, are you sure she will say yes to me? What if something goes wrong? I hate rejections,' said Rohan hitting me with a pillow.

I was in deep sleep when Rohan came and was woken up by his constant chatter about his complicated love life. The only problem in supporting people in love is that they don't sleep and eat, nor do they allow you to eat or sleep either.

'Rohan, do you think I am an astrologer that I can predict these things? I told you yesterday that she obviously loves you. Otherwise why will she take care of you so much? She has better work to do in life.'

'So should I tell her about my feelings today?'

'No. Do one thing. Go visit an astrologist first. See what timing he gives you and ask him which gemstone you should wear on your finger so the stars work in your favour. Then sing some Bhajans and only then go and propose to her,' I said irritatingly from under the blanket.

'Ok fine. I'll do it myself,' Rohan said annoyingly.

I had no option but to get up and comfort him otherwise he would have fucked my brain till it exploded. I made him understand that he had nothing to lose and also told him to act confident in front of her. When it comes to confessing your love for someone, guys always pretend to act macho, but deep inside they are scared to death. I told Rohan to act like his usual self in front of her so that she doesn't suspect anything suspicious. Rohan took my advice seriously and left to meet Riddhima, allowing me to sleep once again. But just when I shut my eyes, he came barging into my room and woke me up, yet again.

'Adi, get up please. I am confused. Which colour shirt should I wear?'

'Wear a swimming costume and go, for all I care, you asshole. But just let me sleep, I beg of you.'

Rohan made a sad face and turned around to leave.

'Stop making me feel guilty. Wear the blue shirt. That colour suits you,' I told him.

Rohan thanked me for my help and left.

'Please don't knock again. Just go and hit a home run. Good luck,' I yelled as he left the room.

Before leaving, Rohan checked himself in the mirror numerous times from all angles—much more than he had in his entire lifetime. He wanted to make Riddhima feel special and was willing to go to any lengths to do that. When your heart begins to work towards another person's happiness, you know you're doing it not for some trifling amusement but for true love. Whenever Rohan felt broken on the inside, all he had to do was turn his head and look at Riddhima who cheered him up without fail. She was the joy of his life and kept him going even in his most trying times. Sometimes when someone new enters your life, the person either becomes just a page of your life or its greatest story. Rohan had decided to meet Riddhim a near her apartment in NIBM and take her out for lunch.

By the time he reached her place, Riddhima was waiting for him near the gate. Just the mere sight of her made him nervous as was now going to meet her with a different intention in mind. He had started loving her and wanted to be a part of her life forever. He always found her beautiful but had never really gathered the courage to tell her that. Plus, he had now started looking at her differently—not so much in the capacity of a friend but someone he could spend the rest of his life with. Riddhima stood next to the lamppost, looking elegant in her red tube top and denims. Her sexy smile added to her beauty. He stopped the bike near her. She sat behind him, keeping her hand on his shoulders for support. If petrol wasn't so expensive, he would have driven her around forever.

'You look good, Rohan. Blue suits you,' Riddhima complemented.

Rohan just smiled and looked into her eyes through the rearview mirror. She glanced back at him and smiled.

'Where are we going?' Riddhima asked.

'Pu La Deshpande Park.'

The park was situated at Sinhagad road. Also known as Friendship Garden, it was built with the idea of recreating an original Japanese garden, giving the city-goers a chance to enjoy its lush green grass cover, providing a visual treat in the early morning. It is well maintained, with an artificial lake, and is home to many rare varieties of birds. There are many trees around and the pathways are barricaded by bamboo sticks on both sides. There are water channels along the path where one can spot many a colourful fish.

Rohan and Riddhima rested on one of the benches and gazed the beauty of the garden without really saying anything to each other.

'Is there anything special today?' Riddhima asked finally breaking the silence between them.

'Yes. But I am not sure how to tell you this.'

'What are you talking about?' she asked turning towards him.

'I had planned to tell you so much today, but now I'm at a complete loss for words. When I'm with you, I can barely talk. You give me butterflies in my tummy. And when I'm away from you, I can barely think about anything but you since you're always on my mind,' Rohan whispered moving closer to her.

'What happened, Rohan? Are you alright?' she blushed.

He felt the heat in his body even in the chilly winter morning. After gaining courage, he finally decided to come to the point and not beat about the bush.

'I want to ask you that…I mean, you know, I want to tell you…how should I…' he stammered.

How the hell do guys ask girls for a one-night stand during their first meeting itself? I am not even able to say 'I have started liking you'. Dammit! he thought.

'Why are you behaving so weirdly?' Riddhima said taking his hand in hers.

Oh God. I am already fucking nervous and by holding my hand, she is making me more nervous. Now I understand why most beautiful girls in the city roam around with nerds who are a complete mismatch for them. It's not because there's something special about them but because they had the guts to speak their heart out, he thought.

'Riddhima, I wanted to tell you that…I…I love the way you care for me. Why do you love me so much?'

Fuck…fuck…fuck. I wanted to tell her that I love her and not ask her why on the earth she loves me so much. She must be thinking what a fattu I am.

Riddhima gave him a wry smile and blushed. She knew what Rohan was trying to convey but the girl inside her didn't allow her to showcase her emotions.

'Just because I told you I love you doesn't mean that I want to be in a relationship with you. I simply told you how I feel. I know you love someone else and it's okay,' she said on purpose just to tease Rohan.

But Rohan took her seriously and avoided broaching the topic now that he knew what her stand was. Little did he know she was merely joking with him. They talked about college, upcoming exams, and what not, but they did not speak a single word about how they felt for each other. Though Rohan had even saved a message in his folder that he wanted to send to her after his proposal, there was no way he could send it now. Riddhima kept forcing him to tell her the secret for which he had asked to meet her since she too wanted to hear him confess his love for her. But Rohan did not broach the topic again for the fear of rejection. She was walking on air knowing she actually meant something to someone.

'WHAAAAT, you came home without telling her? Are you serious?' I asked him when he returned home and told me everything.

He simply nodded and avoided looking at me. I became furious at him, not because he was unable to confess his love to her but because he had disturbed my sleep early morning yet again and had still not been able to tell her about his true feelings.

'How can you? Firstly tell me, who the hell proposes to a girl so early in the morning? You are not going for a morning walk, dammit! You are proposing to a girl. It's not your bloody office where you have to mark your entry at sunrise,' I yelled.

'Just when I was about to confess my love for her, she said that just because she loved me didn't mean she wanted to be in a relationship with me,' he said choking up.

'Girls will be girls. Come on bro, I am assuring you that she loves you. She might have just done that to tease you,' I said cheering him up.

I advised Rohan to try flirting with Riddhima through text messages to see her response. Free or low cost SMS service and social networking sites are a boon to those who are shy to ask girls out in person. They are the ones who make the optimum use of technology. It's quite possible that the guy who doesn't even speak with girls in college is the one who sends maximum friend requests and messages through such sites and is bloody good at it as well. So why can't we?

I motivated Rohan to give it one last shot.

Rohan thought for a moment and sent her a text message: *How many people around you call you by your name?*

Riddhima replied within a few minutes: *Many. Why?*

Rohan winked and replied within seconds, *There are a lot of people who call you by your name. But there's only one person who can make it sound so damn special and that's me.*

Are you sure? she replied.

100% sure, Rohan replied and crossed his fingers anticipating her next reply.

He jumped on the bed in joy when she replied with a kiss smiley and *Lucky me* written next to it. He replied saying he would do anything to impress her like a princess. Romance adds flavour to our lives and makes us feel alive in a way that nothing else can. Rohan shared his plan with me and asked for my help in making it unforgettable for Riddhima.

Riddhima too felt loved and cared for. She knew that Rohan was a genuine person and meant all that he said. It was going to be the start of something beautiful—something that both were anticipating nervously.

28th December, 2009, Midnight

One should not love when one is left stranded or neglected, but when one is prepared to take on the responsibility. Rohan had left behind all the scraps of his previous relationship and was ready to take on the responsibility of being in a new one. He was nervous in the morning, but after a brief chat with Riddhima, he turned confident and was now ready to take on the world. He had decided to make it so memorable that even his grandchildren would be amused by it, knowing how he had proposed to his love. He told me to bring a few things from the market which I did. We had decided to go to Riddhima's apartment around midnight when no one would disturb us or come in our way.

Once the clock struck twelve, we left from Rohan's home. Rohan had decided to come by car while I drove his bike. I had taken a bag with me that had a paint bucket, a brush, and some colours in it, along with some rose petals. The other material was in Rohan's car. As we reached near her apartment, Rohan signalled me to go ahead showing me the exact location and also reminded me to check if her balcony lights were off. Her balcony was visible from the lane under her apartment. I gave him a thumbs up sign indication the lights were indeed off and also looked around to make sure no one was watching me. Marking the location from where she could see clearly from her balcony, I removed the paint and the colours from my bag and started my work. Once done, I called Rohan to drive down and he halted the car at a perfect spot.

'Have you done it properly?' he asked.

'Rest assured,' I said.

I opened the back door of the car and removed the other material, placing it in such a way that Riddhima couldn't see it from the balcony. We kept our fingers crossed and took a deep breath before taking the next step.

'All set?' Rohan asked me.

I replied in the affirmative and hid myself behind the tree. My presence could have made her nervous as I had never met her in person. Rohan went inside the car and called Riddhima.

'Rohan...is everything okay?' she asked looking at the time in her watch.

'Yes. Come to your balcony,' Rohan said looking above through the window of his car.

'Why?' Riddhima asked in a confused tone.

The balcony lights came on the next minute. Riddhima came and stood in the balcony. She looked down and saw Rohan's car parked on the opposite side of the gate. He waved at her from inside his car and said confidently:

'Riddhima, I don't know whether you will like it or not, but I wanted to make you feel special. I am lucky to have you in my life. Whenever I needed you, you stood by me and helped me overcome many obstacles. Today is the perfect time to express my feelings to you. We have been best friends since long time now and know everything about each other. I think we should take our friendship a step ahead. If we can be good friends, then we can be good lovers too. What do you think?'

Riddhima was dumbstruck! It all seemed like a dream to her. She pinched herself to make sure it was really happening.

She smiled looking at Rohan and whispered over the phone, 'Rohan...Do you really mean it?'

Rohan turned on the ignition and stepped on the accelerator. The car moved ahead to reveal a message that was hidden beneath it, written in paint and surrounded by rose petals.

'I love you my princess. Make me unofficially yours.'

She was left speechless. He really had gone to great lengths to make her feel like a princess. Riddhima's happiness knew no limits and she felt like announcing it to the world that her love was proposing to her at the stroke of midnight under her apartment.

Before she could even react, she received a message on her mobile from Rohan.

Getting to know you over these last few months has changed my life. I'm happier than I have ever been, and I owe that joy to you. Before I realized your love, there was emptiness in my heart that at times seemed to consume me, that threatened to break me—but now my life is full of meaning and purpose. I can see my future more clearly now—you are the light in the dark that guides my steps to where I want to be. When the entire world was once overcast by subtle shades of gray, you brought vibrant colours into my life. There are no words that I can speak, no song that I can sing, and no gesture that I can show, to prove my love for you, for the love I have for you has no definition. How can I describe the sheer joy I feel with the very thought of you? How simply hearing your voice causes my heart to beat faster, my pulse to race, and my smile to widen? How can just one person give me so much hope for a future I have always dreamed of having? You have opened my heart and awakened my soul. That is how I know that our love is everlasting. When I look into your eyes—those gorgeous eyes—I see a reflection of my own soul. And in your arms, I know there is no place on earth that I would rather be. I love you. I really love you, Riddhima.

If you too feel the same for me then come down and give me a hug.

Riddhima came down running from her room. The wait for her to come down seemed like a lifetime to Rohan. Sometimes you have to wait for a very long time to find that special person, but it is definitely worth the wait! Rohan and Riddhima both had to wait but they had finally found their forever.

Rohan came out of the car and threw open his arms as soon as he saw Riddhima running towards him. Forgetting the world around them, without caring if someone was watching them, she just hugged him tight and he wrapped his arms around her. It was the longest hug of their lives and neither wanted to let go, having waited to confess their love to each other for so long. When they broke the embrace, Rohan kissed her forehead and said, 'I love you'.

'I love you too,' she said with tears of happiness in her eyes.

Their lips touched softly into the kiss of a lifetime. With one kiss you can surrender yourself so completely to your love. Riddhima had surrendered herself in the passion of the moment.

I had lit a couple of red sky lanterns while they embraced.

I let go of the lanterns as soon as they broke their kiss—much to Riddhima's surprise. I wished both of them good luck for the new beginning and told Rohan to bring the other lanterns from the car. Both of them too lit the lanterns and released them in the sky while making a wish. A wish to remain together forever. A wish to support each other forever until death did them apart. A wish to never lose the spark in their relation until they turn sixty and more.

Uske saath rehte rehte hamein chahat si ho gayi,
Usse baat karte karte hamein aadat si ho gayi.
Ek pal bhi na mile toh ajeeb si becheini rehti hai,
Dosti nibhaate nibhaate hume mohabbat si ho gayi!!
Ab toh Aziz bhi woh hai aur naseeb bhi woh hai,
Duniya ki bheed main kareeb bhi woh hai.
Unki duao se chalti hai zindagi kyonki,
Khuda Bhi woh hai aur taqdeer bhi woh hai!!

You Gave Me a Hangover

28th December, 2009, Mid-day

Have you ever searched for something for hours only to realize that it was lying right in front of you? Many a times we spend all our time searching for an answer that was always known to us. The problem is that we don't believe we can get something that easily, making us doubt its authenticity. Rohan had the same feeling till last night. His true love Riddhima was right next to him but he had never thought about pursuing his relationship with her seriously. Have you ever thought about the number of times we've lost a person just because we didn't have the courage to talk to them in first place? Probably a small chat would have done the trick. But how will one know what the other person feels about you if you don't even give it a shot? We all have that one person in our lives without whom life seems hopeless. Be it your friends or the love of your life, both enter your life in unexpected ways and prove love's existence in strange ways. Rohan's friend Virat and the love of his life, Riddhima, both had entered his life in such a way.

It was already noon and Rohan was still snoring in his bed. In the midst of planning to throw their 'Relationship Party' in the evening at Riddhima's home, they had talked all night over the phone and didn't realize when night had turned into day.

Rohan woke up the moment his phone beeped. It was a message from Riddhima.

The thought of us being together forever made me stay up all night. Missing you so much.

It's always lovely to hear someone misses you. It makes you feel loved. Rohan got ready within a few minutes and left to meet Riddhima after eating his breakfast. They wanted to buy stuff for the party in the evening. He picked Riddhima up and went to D-mart. It's not often that Rohan took interest in grocery shopping but like they say, love makes you do unimaginable things.

'Are we done?' Rohan asked after an hour of shopping.

'Yes,' Riddhima said struggling to hold the many bags in her hands.

Rohan took a few of them and opened the door of the car for her. She gave him a smile and kissed him on the cheek.

'Anything else, madam?' Rohan said bowing down in front of her like a chauffeur.

'Nothing driver,' she chuckled sitting inside as Rohan shut the door after her.

Rohan held her hands and as he drove the car to her apartment. He parked the car and Riddhima was about to move out when Rohan pulled her towards him. She closed the door and tilted towards Rohan.

'Rohan…what are you doing? Someone might see us here.'

The tension in her voice was evident. She looked around to see if someone was watching them.

'No one will disturb us. All the glasses are tinted black,' Rohan exclaimed.

He held her face in his hands and moved closer. She knew he wanted to kiss her but she wanted to play hard to get card. Rohan tried pinning her hands and holding her down to kiss, but she kept getting away. Finally, he grabbed her hair and pulled her gently towards him. He brought his lips close to hers and touched them gently. He tried to enter her mouth with his tongue but she kept resisting. As the kissing grew more intense, she finally gave in and let his tongue explore her mouth. Their tongues played with each other until Rohan pulled away for a moment to look into her eyes. They smiled at each other and he again lip-locked her.

After their first intense smooch, Riddhima reluctantly

broke free from his grip, reminding him it was getting late and that he better leave.

'The way you look at me with those adorable eyes of yours makes me melt inside. You have made me realize what love is all about,' Riddhima whispered as she got out of the car.

If you have a partner who not only loves you, but respects your feelings and understands your emotions, you don't need to bother about what people say. A single word of appreciation is all that matters. Rohan kept looking at her till she was out of sight. He then turned around his car and left for his place.

28th December, 2009, Evening
Coffee Café Day, Baner

'I am going to miss you for an entire week. I am so used to your irritating voice that it's impossible now to live without you, even for a day,' Virat said sipping his coffee.

Virat and Kavya were at Baner's Coffee Café Day, chit-chatting over steaming hot cups of coffee. Though there were many eateries on Baner Road, she preferred to go to a coffee shop every time since the place was relatively quiet and you could hear the other person speak. They had ordered snacks and were gossiping about their Virat's love life.

'Enjoy your freedom with your girlfriend. Once I am back,

I am not going to leave you both alone even while you're having sex,' Kavya teased him by poking him in the arm.

'If that's the case, I better don't tell you my honeymoon room number,' Virat added.

You are never true friends unless you chat about useless and irrelevant topics. Kavya and Virat discussed every silly topic under the sun, but whenever Kavya had to go to her hometown, it made Virat sad and lonely. Kavya was leaving around night-time, alone, as her parents had already left a day before. She was going to return after a week and there were chances that her return might get prolonged depending on the health of her grandmother, which had turned critical in the past few days. Hence, Virat and Kavya had decided to spend some time together since they were not going to see each other for long.

'You are supposed to reach your friend's party, right?' she asked.

'Yeah. Rohan and Riddhima are finally dating each other. So it's party time. I am going directly from here,' Virat stated.

'Cool. Everyone is finding true love these days. Is there some discount offer going on?' Kavya joked.

'Should I laugh?' Virat smirked.

'As if I care,' Kavya said dismissively.

The waiter served the Chocolate Brownie that they had ordered and both pounced on it like they were Tom and Jerry. Within seconds, it was over and they laughed looking at the chocolate on each other's faces. Kavya glanced at

Virat as she licked the last bits of chocolate on the spoon. Suddenly, a feeling of emptiness overcame her as she realized she would be staying away from Virat for more than a week.

'Virat…tell me, frankly…What all will you miss about me?' she asked in a low tone.

Virat was busy on his mobile phone. Before he could answer Kavya, he got a call from Rohan enquiring about his whereabouts.

'I am on my way. Reaching in an hour. Sorry buddy, I got stuck in traffic.'

Virat made up an excuse since he wanted to spend some time with Kavya. There was no way he could have reached NIBM in an hour during evening hours. Virat kept his phone aside and asked Kavya to repeat her question.

'You should be paying more attention. I simply asked what will you miss about me in my absence,' Kavya said in an irritated tone.

'I will miss everything about you. You are a single piece in this whole world. They stopped making friends like you a long time ago,' Virat answered.

He got up from the couch and gave Kavya a tight hug to show how much she meant to him. Soon, they decided it was time to leave. They walked to the parking lot, with Virat guiding her to the car. He opened the door and realized that he had not locked his car.

'How many times do I need to tell you to check whether the doors are locked properly or not? You are so careless,

Virat. Do you realize your car could have been stolen?' Kavya shouted.

They stared at each other for a few seconds and burst out laughing. Kavya always shouted at him for being so careless with his things but he never bothered with it.

'Should I leave?' she asked finally.

'Yeah. Take care and happy journey. Call me once you leave for the station,' he said in a sad tone.

Virat and Kavya were inseparable and whenever they were forced to part from each other for a long period of time, neither took it too well. Both were lucky to have each other in their lives and did not for once take their friendship for granted. Though Kavya was leaving for a fortnight, Virat was pained by the temporary separation since he was so used to her company. They spent most of their hours together and it would be difficult for Virat to lead a life in her absence, even for a few days. Virat waved back at Kavya from inside his car. He then scrolled down his message folder to the SMS he had received from Rohan a while ago giving Riddhima's address. He then headed straight to her place.

'Please bring some candles along,' Riddhima asked Rohan over the phone. He was on his way to her home.

They had made preparations to spend a perfect evening together, complete with music and drinks. As he took out his mobile phone from his pocket, he glanced at the wallpaper on the screen which had Riddhima's picture. He had changed his wallpaper to her picture that very morning itself. He typed her a message:

You will look ravishing covered in my kisses. You always ask me whether you are better than my ex or not, so let me tell you the truth today—no one can be compared to you, my love. I love you so much and I wonder to myself why? You know what they say—when you know why you like someone, it's a crush and when you can't think of a reason or explanation, its love.

He read the message once again before pressing the send button. He re-read it twice and then thought of deleting it. After all, it had only been a day since they started seeing each other. He feared what Riddhima would think about him. But the best conversations are those that never take place, like the messages that we never send.

Rohan reached Riddhima's house and knocked on the door. She let him inside, though something had changed this time; earlier he used to visit to learn French and now he was here to teach her how to French kiss, if the stars favoured him. He called Virat to ask him where was and how long he'd take to reach.

Virat was about to reach Rohan's place when suddenly he took a U-turn in high speed. The other cars came to a halt the moment Virat took the sudden turn and sped away. While he was waiting for the signal to turn green, he received a message. He immediately called on the unknown number and before the person on the other end could explain the whole thing, he ended the call. Suddenly, he felt numb—like his whole world had come crashing down. He couldn't believe his ears. It was, by far, the worst news of his life.

He stepped on the accelerator and drove the car at full speed. He informed Rohan that he couldn't make it as he had to see Kavya urgently. He parked the car outside a hospital and rushed in. As he made his way towards the main entrance to the hospital, he realized he had not locked the car.

Kavya's words reverberated in his ears: *'How many times should I tell you to check whether the doors are locked properly or not? You are so careless, Virat.'* As he thought about how she had lectured him for being careless, tears rolled down his eyes.

He thought about all the crazy moments they had spent together. He remembered their long drives and the way she tickled him while he drove. She was the password to his life like he was to hers. Without each other for support, they were left clueless. Virat's mind had gone completely blank and he didn't know what to do. In such situations, Kavya would be the first person he would've called, but who should he call in her absence? Kavya had been admitted in the hospital and as he stood by the door to her hospital room, he missed that support of hers he had always taken for granted.

With heavy steps, he walked towards the hospital bed. It was heartbreaking for him to see his best friend in the hospital, someone he was laughing with just a few hours ago. It was heartbreaking to see such a jolly person lying in a hospital bed hooked up to machines. It was hard for him to imagine that she was the same Kavya who used to tease him every now and then. She was the same Kavya who would wipe the tears off his eyes. The same Kavya was now lying lifeless on the bed. He felt uneasy looking at her in that condition. The doctors had kept her under observation and didn't tell Virat why she had been admitted. Never in his wildest dreams had he imagined something so heartbreaking. Kavya's parents were informed and Virat dealt with the rest of the formalities. He tried to keep a check on his emotions and knew that if he let a single tear flow, he would never be able to stop. He managed to remain composed, at least until he got back in his shower where his tears could mix with the water and nobody would know. He sat outside the room, begging for this to be nothing but a dream. He desperately wanted to collapse into someone's arms. He had told Mehak about it all and she rushed to join him, leaving all her work aside.

When someone you love, someone you wished to spend your life with, departs unexpectedly, it leaves you completely drained—physically and mentally. Virat wanted to scream in pain but tried to gather courage since he knew Kavya needed him. For all the times she had stood by him, it was time for him to payback.

A few hours earlier...
Coffee Café Day, Baner

Virat waved Kavya goodbye and drove away. Kavya stood there, alone and helpless, with different emotions running through her head. Though she was going away for a fortnight, it felt like a year to her. She remembered how he made her so happy and carefree. As much as we wish for things to stay the same, uncertainty is an inevitable part of our life. Kavya had thought of celebrating her birthday with Virat and Mahek, but if she had to stay for long in her hometown, she might have to celebrate it alone, without her friends. This made her more upset and she stood there looking at his car until it disappeared from her sight. She just hoped to return before her birthday and wished for a miracle which would prolong her stay in Pune.

Just when her mind was buzzing with a million questions, she got a call from her mom.

'Yes, mom. I have packed my bags. Dad will be come to pick me up, right?' she said walking on the pavement trying to hail an autorickshaw.

'Yes, beta. He will be there to pick you up before your

train reaches. Don't worry. Now, where are you? There is so much noise in the background,' her mom asked.

'I had come to meet Virat and now I'm looking for an auto to go home. He was getting late and so he left in a hurry. He would've dropped me, but I told him not to.'

Since there were very few autos around, she was having difficulty finding one to take her home. The few that she tried to hail whizzed past her without stopping. Upon spotting an auto on the other side of the road, she put the call on hold and screamed at the top of her lungs, 'Chaloge bhaiya?' The auto driver turned the meter down and told her to come to his side of the road.

'Mom, I've got an auto. I will call you once I reach home. Take care. Bye,' Kavya said signalling the auto driver to wait for a moment.

'Ok, beta. Take care. And don't talk to strangers on the train. Take everything you need with you.'

'Don't irritate me, mom,' Kavya smirked and hung up.

She disconnected the call and saw an unread message pop up on her mobile screen. She read it while hurriedly crossing the road. It was Mehak: *Hey, Babe. Happy journey and do miss us. We will miss you, especially….*

Before she could read the complete message, a tempo coming at her at full speed knocked her down. All of a sudden, traffic came to a standstill and a huge crowd gathered around her. Before she could realize what had actually happened, she felt a sharp pain all over her body. She was lying in a pool of blood, with injuries all over her body. The tempo driver had feared a collision with another bike coming from the wrong lane, so he had turned his vehicle around, only to crash into Kavya. Some people started abusing the tempo driver while some took his side saying it was not his fault and just an accident. Whoever's fault it was, the bottom-line was that Kavya was lying on the road soaked in blood.

She couldn't move even an inch of her body. She was seriously wounded and had sustained injuries on the head and face. Her nose was bleeding and her legs were badly bruised. No one around her bothered to call an ambulance or cared to pick her up and rush her to the hospital. She could see some bikers driving by on the other lane and tried to scream for help but no sound escaped her lips. The crowd kept watching her as she floundered in pain. Each minute seemed like a lifetime. She wished she could call Virat but even her hands felt lifeless and she could not lift them up.

'Help…help…someone call the ambulance,' someone screamed.

Another person called for the ambulance and told them to rush to the spot looking at the grave nature of her injuries. She was taken to Mid Point hospital and two people from the crowd volunteered to go with her. One of them checked the 'last dialled' list in her mobile and informed everyone she had called in the recent past. Virat and her mom were two of them. She was immediately admitted in the emergency and was kept under observation till she regained consciousness.

All her happiness had come to an abrupt end. It had put a sudden stop on her life, something she hadn't expected. All the lives associated with her were shattered. Virat rushed to the hospital once he was told what had happened.

Every time Virat and Kavya met, they made each other laugh. Every time she smiled, it made the sun come out from behind the clouds of his heart. It seemed impossible to live without her. But now he was left with only hope. A hope to smile together again, a hope to tease each other again, a hope of her shouting at him for not keeping things in place, hope a for walking together again around the college campus.

Sometimes, life is so unpredictable; you meet a person and everything goes along at its own smooth pace. The next moment, you get the news that the person is fighting for their life and it renders you miserable and heartbroken.

Mid Point Hospital, Aundh

Misfortune flooded the lives of Kavya's parents. Upon hearing the news of her daughter's tragic accident, they were shocked. Waiting outside Kavya's hospital room, Virat was lost his thoughts.

I *should have dropped you. I shouldn't have left you alone.*

What if no one would have helped you? I wouldn't have forgiven myself my entire life. I had planned a surprise for you on your birthday. Tell me, this is all a big joke and that you will get up and come along for a movie and cut the cake too. I owe you a drink, too, remember? Ok, don't show up for the birthday party but please get up. Hold my hand and never let go. Just give me one more chance to tell you how much you mean to me. I am ready to fight with the almighty to bring you back. I am ready to bribe him too, but just… come back. I can't see you like this in a hospital bed, cold and numb. Please pull through; I know you can make it. Don't make me cry. Are you so angry with me? My life is nothing without you. There are other ways to tease me, why choose this one? Whether I appreciate you or not, you're always in my heart and I need you to comfort me. I am not going to let you shut your eyes forever. Our friendship can't be so short. How can I say goodbye so soon?

A Different Kind of Pain

Mid Point Hospital, Aundh

Virat had never thought something like this would happen and that he would end up missing Kavya so much. He had never asked God for anything before in his entire life, but this situation forced him to pray for Kavya. He closed his eyes and prayed to God for her speedy recovery. He wouldn't have minded switching places with Kavya and be the one suffering. In fact, he would have accepted it happily had it meant Kavya would be okay. He wanted Kavya back in his life, and was willing to do whatever it took.

Just then he heard Mehak's voice asking, 'Virat, how is Kavya? What happened exactly? Did you inform her parents? What did the doctor say?'

He could tell she was worried about her. She had grown increasingly close with Kavya in the past couple of months and wanted to know if she was doing okay. As soon as he saw

Mahek, he couldn't control himself anymore; he collapsed in her arms, crying like a little baby. He recounted the entire scenario to her and hugged her in dismay.

'Stop crying. Everything will be all right. If you will act weak like this, then who will be her strength?' said Mahek wrapping her arms around him.

'I shouldn't have listened to her. I should have dropped her home even though she kept saying no.'

'Did you inform her parents?' Mehak asked.

Virat nodded and told her that they'll be reaching any moment. How cruel can life be? It was Christmas week and they were sitting in the hospital praying for their friend. So many times we take our life for granted and say 'I wish I could die' or 'I will die if you don't do this and that' without realizing that someday our wish might just come true.

Mahek brought some sandwiches for Virat but he refused to eat. Mahek didn't force him too much since she knew his mind was preoccupied with thoughts of Kavya. Just when she took a seat beside him, they saw Kavya's parents walking towards them. Virat got up from his seat and took them to the ICU where Kavya was admitted. Her mom broke down as soon as she saw her little girl hooked to machines. Her dad went to speak with the doctor to find out how grave her condition was and to complete the necessary formalities as well.

'We will keep her under observation for the next 48 hours. There are many stitches on her legs and she has suffered a severe head injury. There's damage to her brain. Even after she comes back to her senses, she may have partial memory loss or loss of vision. You all need to be strong.'

Silence filled the air for a few seconds until Kavya's dad asked, 'Doctor, will she recover soon?'

The doctor just gave a pat on her dad's shoulder and left. Virat felt like threatening the doctor into treating her properly and giving her the best possible care, but in such situations we forget that doctors are not Gods who can do everything. All they could do was wait for Kavya to come back to life.

They waited impatiently for the hours to pass, holding on to the belief that Kavya would open her eyes and break into a smile, bringing back joy into their world. No one was able to sleep and almost everyone had given up on eating. Each minute made them physically weak. Their only glimmer of hope was that Kavya was responding well to medicines and treatment. Virat was missing her kid-like behaviour and her sweet smile. It hurts when the hand that supports you is suddenly snatched away from your life, leaving you to think what went wrong. Mahek, too, was missing the sweet friend she had found in Kavya. Most hurt in all this were her parents. They couldn't see their daughter covered in bandages and in so much pain. She had been the apple of their eyes and they had always treated her like a princess and always protected her with love and care. Finally, after 24 hours had passed, the doctor approached them with a smile on his face, saying she was out of danger, though unconscious at the moment.

Virat peeped into her room through the little window. *She looks so innocent,* he thought. It seemed as though she was watching a beautiful dream and would open her eyes only once the dream ended. Her body was covered with a bed sheet and different machines were monitoring her heartbeat, blood pressure; and pulse rate, and it scared Virat. He felt helpless, like nothing was in his control. He could take care of a bruise on the knee, but this was above his scope of knowledge. Everytime her heartbeat showed a decline on the monitor, he would break out into a sweat, worried he was losing her. Though he was crying on the inside, he didn't let his real emotions show and kept up a brave front in front of her parents who were crying inconsolably.

It was 3 pm in the afternoon when everyone finally decided to grab something to eat. Right after Mahek had taken a bite of her sandwich, she saw Kavya move slightly. She dropped her sandwich on the ground and rushed to call the doctors. They came rushing to examine her. Kavya was doing everything in her capacity to fight against the odds. As she slowly opened her eyes, everyone stood by her side in eager anticipation. One of the doctors examined her while the nurses assisted him in checking her pulses.

'How are you feeling now?' the doctor asked but Kavya didn't respond.

He repeated his question, 'Kavya, how are you feeling?'

She still gave a blank expression. Everyone got tense. Her parents tried to communicate with her but failed. Her mom broke down in tears again, asking what was wrong. Kavya was struggling to talk.

Virat went closer to her but she didn't even look at him. Her eyes were fixed on the ceiling above.

'Kavya, don't you recognize me? I'm Virat. How are you? We missed you so much. We were so afraid. We thought we had lost you forever. You know, I even prayed to God for the first time in my life for your fast recovery. After all, we have to celebrate your birthday with a bang…'

Kavya still didn't show any reaction to what he was saying. Virat was getting increasingly worried.

'Are you feeling better?' Virat continued asking her but this time, his tone showed traces of tension.

She slowly moved her eyes towards Virat but within a fraction of second, she again looked away.

'There is too much darkness here. I can't see anything. Mom, are you there? I can't see you, Mom. Virat, where are you standing? Is dad here?' she murmured.

The doctor told everyone to wait outside as he questioned Kavya. She was speaking fine but everyone was confused and worried about her reaction. They couldn't control their anxiety and wanted to know what was going on. Though she had woken up, it seemed like she hadn't fully recovered. For a fraction of a second, everyone was happy, but their happiness was temporary. Though there was enough light in the room, she couldn't see. It could mean only one thing... they shuddered to even think about it. The doctors came out in a few minutes and told what they had been trying to avoid. Kavya had lost her vision!

Their world came crashing down. How would Kavya engage with the world now? It seemed like she was struggling with a range of emotions—from shock and anger to sadness and frustration. Her life had lost its colours, except for black, which isn't the most reassuring colour to wake up to. Her parents tried to console Kavya, but somewhere deep down within themselves, they too were bleeding tears of sorrow. Their little princess had lost her vision! They stood beside her, holding one of her hands. Virat couldn't believe this was happening. He couldn't digest the fact that Kavya couldn't see him anymore which meant that they couldn't go around the city on his bike irritating people, they couldn't watch a movie together, and she couldn't tell him which colour t-shirts look better on him. Mahek too was sobbing away in a corner.

Kavya was trying to recollect how the accident exactly happened. She had lost her hope to live. She didn't say anything to anyone and was lost in her own thoughts.

Now what am I supposed to do? How would I cope? Dad was just going to gift me a new bike on this birthday, but now what's the use? How will I go out shopping?

Her family had to finally accept her condition and figure out how they could support her. Kavya felt guilty of putting her parents through so much hurt and pain.

'Mom, now I am just a burden to you guys. It was my time to take care of you in your old age but now you need to take care of me. I have become useless,' Kavya cried.

'No beta. You are still our princess and you will always be. You are not only our daughter but our son too. A child can never be a burden on their parents. Don't stress out. We all are here for you,' her mom reassured her and gave her a tight hug.

'Virat, are you here? Where are you? Come near me,' Kavya added.

Virat cursed the fate that put her through this. The girl who would pinch him, jump on him, and do all kinds of crazy things in the world couldn't see him anymore.

He went closer to her and said, 'Kavya, get well soon. We will go out again and have fun. We will again blow bubbles in the air and trouble everyone on our way. This time, I won't stop you,' Virat said controlling his tears.

Kavya smiled slightly and said, 'But I can't be your security guard anymore.'

Virat couldn't control his emotions anymore and a drop of tear fell on her hand.

'What is this, Virat? Why are you crying? You should be happy that now no one can trouble you to clean your room. Does Mahek know how sloppy you are?'

'Yes, I do,' Mahek said from a distance.

'Oh, Mahek. Sorry, I didn't see you…oh, I mean, hear you,' Kavya said correcting her mistake.

She felt uncomfortable using the word 'see' as it held no value in her life anymore. It was important for everyone to be sensitive and empathetic towards her treatment because the degree of depression Kavya may be overcome by was high. So many times we see blind people around us but never understand their pain and struggle. It's rightly said that we can understand what a person goes through only when we are forced to walk in their shoes. One moment had changed everything.

31st December, 2009, New Year's Eve
Midpoint Hospital, Aundh

Virat had decided to spend New Year's Eve with Kavya at the hospital itself. Doctors had said that she would be discharged within 6 weeks, depending on the rate of her recovery. Looking at her response to the treatment, everyone was happy. The doctors said that if she co-operates and shows the same kind of progress, they could take her home in a month. There was no way that Virat and Mahek would have celebrated their first new year together leaving Kavya alone in a hospital bed. They decided to stay with her and share their happiness with her.

At the stroke of midnight, everyone wished each other and prayed for a better year ahead of them, especially for Kavya's fast recovery. Kavya looked upset and cursed her fate. She remembered how she had done crazy things the last New Year's Eve with Virat.

'I have a surprise for you,' Virat said to Kavya.

'What's that?' Kavya asked.

He removed a letter from his bag and started reading it to her in the presence of the hospital staff and Kavya's parents.

Happy New Year! It's that time again, when we shed the old and welcome the new. We say goodbye to the past and are encouraged by the chance to start again. People disregard and down-talk new years' resolutions because we never keep them anyway. But I am not talking about a resolution to be attempted and discarded. I am taking about a new way life. It's almost a week that you have been here, unaware of what's happening in the world. But I promise that I will be your vision from now onwards. Mahek too wants you to get well soon so that you can go around with her, teasing boys on the road like you used too. She will not let you run away from the happiness that you so deserve. I know what this year was like for you and for all of us. There were some heartbreaks, lost opportunities and broken dreams too. Maybe, there was frustration and anger too. But my dearest friend, where there is life, there is hope. It may not be exactly what you want, but you have the power to change it. Starting with how you see yourself and how you see others. When you know that you are valuable and truly, genuinely, like yourself, that love spreads to everyone around you. I'm not talking about the loud self-confidence that shouts for attention. I mean the quiet confidence that whispers 'I know who I am'. With that type of self-esteem, you dis-empower the words of abuse in your life. You shoot your insecurities down to the ground and you show that hateful voice in your head who's the boss. Your parents, Mahek and I…we all love you. Forever. You are our princess. And don't worry, I will never tell your parents about the stuff we did this year.

Heaven must be looking down over us because they blessed me with you. I know times are tough, but we are each other's strength. I love you so much, my dearest friend, so remember that you are my 'hope' which is the ultimate desire of all human kind. No matter how terrible the tragedies of life, as long as we can catch a glimmer of hope, we can survive life's worst encounters. Promise me, you will never cry and will smile always as that's what makes you beautiful. Whatever may be the situation; you will survive and remain unchanged as we love our Kavya who is as nutty as a fruit cake. Your birthday is nearing and we will celebrate it together like we did last year. Such accidents can't spare the city from our harassment and pagal-panti.

After the letter ended, everyone around broke into a loud applause. In the midst of all the pain she was suffering, Virat's friendship was her only hope. He was sacrificing his social life just for her happiness and just so he could pamper her. Indeed, nothing had changed after Mahek's entry into his life. Mahek was lucky that she had a partner like Virat who was so caring and affectionate towards his loved ones. Virat was equally lucky as he had unconditional support and understanding from his love. Kavya was the luckiest of all as she had both Virat and Mahek in her life.

10th January, 2010
Mid Point Hospital, Aundh

There are two types of pain that we encounter in our lives: One that hurts you and other that changes you. Kavya had encountered the storm of pain but it didn't hurt her, rather it made her strong as a person.

It had almost been a fortnight since Kavya had been admitted and her determination gave her strength everyday. She was getting used to her life a day at a time. The doctors had shifted her from the ICU to a regular room. Her pill intake was reduced as she had recovered partially. Slowly, she had again started smiling even though the pain of the physical wounds was visible on her face. Her smile didn't mean that her life was perfect, but that she appreciated what she had. She was trying to do things on her own though it wasn't always easy for her.

Virat wanted to make her birthday special as Kavya had gone through so much in the past few days and deserved every chance of happiness she got. Kavya's parents had co-operated with Virat who wanted to celebrate her birthday at the hospital like no one would have imagined. He wished her at midnight and came to the hospital early morning with a surprise.

Kavya was sleeping in her room when he tiptoed into the room. Mahek had already decorated the hospital room with a few balloons and ribbons while Kavya was asleep. Though they knew that Kavya would not be able to see the decoration, they didn't care. The cake was ready on the folding table that Virat had got with him. The visitors who were sitting outside peeped into the room to see what was happening. Virat played the birthday song on his mobile and Kavya woke up to a shock.

Everyone, including Kavya's parents, clapped and cheered for her.

'Mom, are Virat and Mahek here?' Kavya asked.

'Yes.'

The birthday song continued and Kavya felt extremely special. She couldn't believe all the arrangement her friends had done just to make her feel special. Her mom told her that her friends had brought the cake and decorated the room with balloons and ribbons.

Tears rolled down her eyes and she asked, 'Virat, why you are doing so much for me? You people are making me feel so special, as if I am going to die in few months,' she winked.

'You will never change, right?' Mahek said and continued, 'Don't say that ever again.'

'You want me to?'

'Never.'

Virat helped her cut the cake with a knife and they once again sang Happy Birthday in chorus. Kavya fed the first piece of the cake to her parents followed by Virat and Mahek. Even the nurses and doctors joined later and wished her well. She had won the hearts of the doctors too with her innocent smile.

'Kavya, get ready for the surprise,' Virat announced.

He opened the play list in the mobile and played the byte he had recorded over the past few days. The recording had one message each from her parents, Virat and Mahek. He had edited the unclear part out and had added soft music in the background. Once played, it sounded like a song.

Virat began, *Kavya everyone loves you and this is just a small token of love from our side. Here are the messages that everyone wants to give on your birthday…*

Mahek: *Hey Kavya, a very happy birthday to you! Fun is waiting for us outside. Get well soon. We are the kind of friends who, when in a hospital together, would race our wheelchairs up and down the corridor and halls yelling 'Gotta go'.*

Virat: *It's a special day in your life. Happy birthday. I am luckyto have a friend who always seems to make me laugh at my lowest point, just want to say thanks for knowing what I need. Everyone should have a best friend like you. But they shouldn't steal mine. You are my best friend. I love you.*

Mom: *Happy birthday, beta. What should I say? Our home is lonely without you. There is no one at home who makes a mess of the room, throwing clothes here and there. Even our maid goes home early nowadays. Sometimes, you are mad at me. Sometimes, I am mad at you. But I still enjoy playing the part of your mother as we would really go mad without you. Come home soon and bring it back to life.*

Dad: *Wish you a warm birthday, my princess. As you father, I have always secretly hated the fact that you are growing up because I know that every passing moment brings me one step closer to the day when I will have to give your hand to another man. Daddy loves you, sweetheart.*

By the time the recording ended, there was a huge smile on Kavya's face. She felt like she was able to see everyone. She was able to visualize their expressions. It was probably one of her best birthdays, even though it was celebrated in a hospital room. Kavya thanked everyone for their warm wishes through such a lovely medium. If you have people like them around you, life is awesome. Such incidents make you realize that money and success are nothing. It's the love and affection from your family and friends that matters the most.

29th January, 2010

Friendships are what make us strong when we feel weak, happy when we feel sad, and comforted when we feel alone. Virat and Kavya's relationship had proved that you don't need a boyfriend or a girlfriend to be happy, all you need is a good friend who is always putting a smile on your face. Mahek and Kavya's relationship had also proved that two girls can be best friends and wish for each other's betterment, no matter where life takes you. One month had passed since the accident and Kavya was finally getting discharged. Her dad had gone back home while her grandmother who was in a critical condition all that while had passed away. To perform the rituals, her dad had left Pune and was supposed to be back after two weeks. We all had a brief talk with the doctors and they had given a green signal to take her home, but they told us to take care of her as for the first time she was going to witness the outside world without her eyes. They had even told us that in such situations, the patient doesn't react very well and may take out her frustration on someone. So we had to be prepared for it.

'Wear this whenever you go out,' the doctor said giving

her a pair of dark glasses as she got up from her bed.

'Ok, doctor,' Kavya smiled.

'Thank god she didn't ask for a Ray Ban,' Virat joked.

Kavya tried to pinch him in the direction where she heard his voice but missed him by a whisker. She got a bit annoyed and Virat sensed her agitation. He purposely went closer to her in the direction of her hands so that she could pinch him.

'See; don't think that if I can't see then I won't be able to trouble you,' Kavya said with a smile on her face.

Virat held her hand and felt a bit uneasy looking at Kavya's condition. A girl, who was so colourful and lively, who made everyone around her happy and always took care of everyone, needed support today to even get out of her bed. It was commendable on Virat and Mahek's part that they had been with Kavya every moment since the last one month and had never made her feel alone.

Kavya's mom made her sit in Virat's car and Virat drove the car towards her home. Kavya sat expressionless in the car as she couldn't see anything outside the window. Mahek cracked some jokes to lighten her mood. As they reached her home, Kavya asked Virat to take her to her room.

'Please, take me in front of the mirror,' Kavya said.

Virat did as was told without asking her any questions. Kavya stood in front of the mirror and stared at it.

She gave a little smile to Virat and said, 'I just wanted to see how I look after an accident. I was imagining what the mirror would show. My cuts, dark circles under my eyes and the stick that I am holding?'

The hardest things to come to terms with had been not being able to see her own reflection in the mirror. She felt like she had lost her identity.

'Don't stress yourself, out,' Virat said trying to console her. He could understand the mental trauma and crisis of identity she was going through.

'It's so much harder to feel sexy and attractive when I have no idea what clothes I am putting on, or how my mascara looks,' Kavya continued.

Virat made her sit down on the bed and held her hand. It was a difficult phase in their life but Virat knew that he was her courage. He too, had undergone all the pain, mentally, in the last one month though he didn't show it to anyone. Mehak too had to sacrifice a lot over past the few days for Kavya. They both loved Kavya and were ready to spend the rest of their lives making her happy.

Kavya had a habit of switching her TV on as soon as she sat on the bed in her room. But now even that was not possible. She tried to recollect where everything was placed in her room and made her way around the room, touching everything on the way. But when she wakes up in the morning and opens her eyes, there would be nothing but endless darkness.

Those little things that everyone takes for granted are the ones that make life impossible as a blind person—like pouring boiling water to make a cup of tea or even sending a message through your mobile. Every day she grieved for her independence and the person she was before. And it was not just her sight that was gone, even her college life had abruptly come to an end. She relied on her parents and friends completely for everything—from reading messages to shopping. She just couldn't shake off the feeling of being trapped inside her own body.

Old habits die hard, but Kavya was determined to let go of her past and build a strong future. Gradually, she started walking alone around her home and Mahek, being a girl, helped her a lot with things she couldn't talk to her parents about. Virat had promised her that he would never let the fun die in their relationship and he stood by his words. After a week of being discharged, he regularly took Kavya out for a walk in the garden would dutifully describe the surroundings to her—how the children played, oldies jogged and couples kissed.

Day by day, Kavya started feeling better and the presence of her family and friends made her life beautiful in its own way. She too loved all the attention she got. The threads of their friendship had strengthened even more and they were her strength in the true sense of the word. Every moment spent with them motivated her and gave a hope to live a new life all over again. To enjoy the new life as she did before. To make everyone happy around her.

Life is too short to cry over what is lost; Kavya made it the motive of her life to spread happiness around her. She did miss seeing the clouds in the bright blue sky and the stars twinkle at night. She would run her hands over the faces of people she met so that she could visualize their faces in her head. At times, she thought being blind was a good thing in a way. That way, she didn't have to see all the ugliness that's penetrated into our world. She now saw the world through Virat and Mahek's eyes.

Trust Me, I'm Freaking Serious!

9th February, 2010
Virat's Apartment

In life, everyone meets that one person they can talk to about anything. For Virat, that person was Kavya. Some people think a friend is somebody you've known forever. But it's never like that. It's really about who stood by you through everything. Virat and Kavya didn't even know each other a few years back but today they meant everything to each other. Many even thought that they loved each other until Mahek entered Virat's life.

Virat was sitting in his room and was flipping through his childhood album with a glass of beer in his hand. After Kavya's accident, he had started feeling alone though he always tried to keep himself busy. Even in the midst of it all this, he was missing his parents. He kept thinking if something like this would have happened to him, who would have been his moral support. Kavya's parents supported and loved her like anything. Virat felt depressed thinking about it and missed the fatherly touch of his dad and the motherly care of his mom. Though his uncle supported him financially and treated him like a son, no one can replace the love of parents.

As he was flipping through the albums, his phone buzzed. It was Rohan.

'Where have you been these past few days?' You've hardly come on Gtalk.'

'I told you, I was busy at the hospital. My friend is admitted there.'

Rohan had tried reaching Virat a couple of times on phone, but Virat hardly ever responded. Virat had told him that once Kavya was discharged from the hospital, he would meet him and his love Riddhima.

'You have still not met Riddhima. When are you meeting us? And how is Kavya?'

'She is fine. I will meet you guys soon. Anyway, I thought since you now have a girlfriend, you won't get any time to meet your friends. That is what generally happens,' Virat smirked.

They talked for some time and then Virat started to watch a movie on his laptop. He just wanted to get over his feeling of loneliness. Mahek was busy and so he thought a movie would help.

When your relationship goes through some crisis and you're still able to sustain it, your relationship becomes more powerful than ever before.

Sometimes, the strongest of all relationships start out with a small friendship and work its way up. Mahek and Virat's relationship had started with a friendship though it had been intentionally planned so by Kavya. However, Rohan and Riddhima's friendship was never intentional. Though Rohan was in a relationship with Zoya, it was nearly impossible for Riddhima to forget Rohan as she loved him and that love had made a huge impact on her life. Virat and I, together, made Rohan realize the value of her love and he was extremely happy being in a relationship with her. Sometimes, he did remember Zoya, and whenever that happened, I had to travel from Mumbai to Pune just to make him understand that it's over. After all, he treated me more as a friend than a brother. More importantly, he didn't regret his decision of choosing Riddhima as his life partner.

Virat had been stressed since the last few weeks and needed to take rest. He didn't realize when he fell asleep while watching the movie. Suddenly, the bell rang and he got up. It was Mahek. He was surprised to see her at that hour of the day.

'Did you bunk your classes?' Virat asked.

'Yes. Because I want to make out with you right now. And there is a reason behind it.'

Before Virat could answer, she pushed him against the

wall. He stared at her for a few moments, and suddenly the air filled with tension. He leaned back and his hand accidentally fell into a bowl of ketchup kept on the table next to the wall. Mahek licked the sauce from his fingers and the sensation of her touch made his body tickle.

She bit his palms softly and licked his wrist. Her hands came up and grasped his bicep firmly, pushing up his sleeve as her tongue licked the inside of his elbow. She began to make soft moaning sounds and he watched her, hypnotized, eyes wide, unable to pull back from her. Her lips moved swiftly from his elbow to his neck, and he felt the touch of her hot breath on his cold skin. He slowly removed her top exposing her skin. She was trying to unbuckle his belt. She became more furious with every attempt. He pushed her against the wall and removed his belt. She pulled down his pants and underpants, and brought him closer to herself. He let his gaze explore her flawless skin and continued kissing her all over, making her moan in delight. He held her by her hair and bit her neck. She threw her head back and cried out in pleasure.

'Did you come here to tell me something or just to make out?' Virat asked teasing her.

'Yes.'

'So tell me. What is it?'

'How do you know Rohan? Do you know him personally or did you two ever meet?' Mahek asked, looking in his eyes.

'Kind of. I had met him on a random blog on some

blogger's website. I liked his views and had thus added him on my Gmail account. Then gradually, we started chatting. But what happened?'

'So you've never met?'

'Yes. The first time we met was because I needed some information regarding an orphanage.'

'Never through Orkut or Facebook?' Mehak continued asking questions.

'Mahek, you know I am not on Orkut. And forget Facebook. I don't understand anything about it. You think I am hiding something from you?' Virat asked in frustration and pushed her away from him.

Facebook had just been launched and not many people had created accounts on it.

'It just slipped my mind that you are not on Orkut. So you have just met once?'

'You are acting like CID,' he said raising his voice.

'Answer me,' she asked again.

'Ok, let me tell you everything. We started talking casually on Gtalk. He used to tell me about his love life and his ex-girlfriend, Zoya. But then I told him that he should move on and now, he is dating Riddhima. He was confused about the decision so at that time I met him along with his cousin, Aditya. In fact, I was going to meet him on the same day the accident took place. Remember I told you I was going to meet a friend but you didn't know him? It's the same guy.'

'Oh, now I get it. Did you ever tell him about me?' Mahek said looking anxious.

'Probably a few times, I had told him I am in love and was going to propose to my love. But I never mentioned your name. You know, I don't reveal such things because I'm afraid of losing people. But will you tell me what happened with him and why you are asking about him?'

'Thank God, you never mentioned my name to him. I was so afraid that I came running to ask you,' said Mahek breathing a sigh of relief.

'Why?'

'Because he happens to be my cousin.'

Virat immediately got up from his bed. He couldn't believe what he had heard. There was pin-drop silence in the room with both of them staring at each other. He reconfirmed whether he had heard her correctly or not. Mahek nodded in agreement. Virat's face turned deathly white. It was nothing but a horrifying dream. He tried to recollect all his past discussions with Rohan but still couldn't remember him saying anything about Mahek. Nor could he remember Rohan mentioning that he had a sister. This came as a real shocker to him. He felt like he had been caught in a crime.

'I don't remember Rohan mentioning it.'

'Why are you getting so restless?'

'What the fuck do you mean restless? Obviously it's come as a shock to me. God dammit, he is your brother. How did you come to know that he talks to me?' he stammered.

'Keep calm. And he is not my first cousin. He is my cousin Mama's son. So in reality he's a distant relative. We do meet sometimes and share a good bond but I'm surprised your topic never came up whenever I met him. Obviously, he couldn't ask me directly whether I was dating someone or not. Neither did I tell him. Sometimes, he comes to our place and we have a good time. My family is a bit orthodox and I am not comfortable sharing our relationship with my family or Rohan so soon, not until we're done with our education. Today, I saw him talking on the phone and he was taking your name and even Kavya's. He is staying with us tonight. Then when he went to the washroom after sometime, I took his cell phone and luckily it was unlocked. I checked the number he had last dialled and it was you. Then I came running to you.'

Virat was speechless and felt like banging his head against the wall. He was confused whether he should thank his fate that he didn't show her pictures or reveal anything about her to Rohan or curse his fate that Mahek was Rohan's cousin. One thing he was sure about was that although Rohan would get upset in the beginning after knowing everything, he won't stand in the way of their relationship. He knew Rohan liked him as a person and somewhere he thought he should tell Rohan everything rather than hiding the truth from him as it would hurt him more later on. He gave it a thought and said,

'I think we should tell him. He trusts me and he won't tell anything at home. Trust me.'

'No, that's impossible. Please. If my parents come to know then they will cut all my freedom away. They will doubt me continuously, even when I going to a friend's place. We should first complete our education. Please, understand. After all he is my brother,' she panicked.

'Do you know about his current girlfriend?'

'No. He didn't tell me. But I had met his previous girlfriend Zoya. Rather, he had to introduce her because I had seen them together, hand in hand, when I was with my friends. She is a nice girl. We talk occasionally,' Mahek exclaimed.

Sometimes, it's hard to face things you have no control over. Virat was bold enough to confront Mahek's cousin, Rohan. Some say love is blind, but love is challenged in all senses. Because no matter how hard you try, it will always surprise you. Pleasant ones or shocking ones. Virat couldn't categorize this surprise. Mahek had told him such things about Rohan's previous girlfriend Zoya and their relationship that it sent shivers down his spine. He digested the fact that Mahek was Rohan's cousin and was ready to face it with courage but whatever she said about Zoya was unbelieveable. Some things in life are better left unexplained. Virat had already starting planning for a double surprise shocker on Valentine's Day for his friend and future brother-in-law Rohan.

Candy Crush My Heart!

11th February, 2010

'Aadi, she won't be here on Valentine's Day. She will meet me for a few hours but since we can't go on a date together, we are celebrating it today evening. But I just don't know how to make it special for her. Please, please tell me what to do,' Rohan pleaded with me.

I was in Pune during the Valentine's week for my friend's marriage and was staying at Rohan's home. Rohan and his family were spending a few days at his cousin aunt's place in Aundh but Rohan returned home early as I was coming. He had told his parents he has some official work to do. The only person who knew the real reason why Rohan was coming back home early because of me was Mehak. I had never interacted with them before, because Rohan was my Masi's son and they were his father's relatives. So Mahek and I were not really related as such.

He seemed confused about how he should celebrate his first Valentine's Day with Riddhima. She had some extra classes to attend on the actual Valentine's Day, so they decided to celebrate it early. Anyway, when your Valentine is with you, the day doesn't hold importance and even Friendship's Day could mean Valentine's Day to you. It's more about the feelings that two individuals share and how passionate they are about each other.

'Keep it simple. The simplicity in your love and affection towards her is more important. I have an idea. Leave it to me. I will make it memorable for you,' I assured him.

Rohan had decided to meet Riddhima in the evening and I still had a few hours to arrange everything. For his part, I told him to keep it simple yet special.

'Listen, go on a short drive with her first. I will buy you a CD of romantic songs and you can play them in your car while you drive to your chosen destination. I am sure she will love it. Later on, take her for a romantic dinner to an amazing restaurant. I will check online deals for you so that the meal doesn't drill a hole in your pocket. Finally, to end the evening on a perfect note, park your car on some lonely road while returning and express your love to her with a soft kiss,' I said taking a deep breath after narrating the entire plan to him.

I arranged for the CD and bought a deal on Groupon for a meal for two at 50% off at a restaurant in Koregaon Park. The restaurant had rooftop dining where you could get a view of the entire city. *Rohan better treat me for getting him such a great deal,* I thought to myself. Every time a guy takes a girl out on a date, somewhere in some corner of his mind, he's calculating how much the meal would cost him, even if he has a credit card with him. Rohan was happy not only because he was taking Riddhima out on a date to one of the best restaurants in the city but also because he was going to pay only half the price. Rohan was all geared up for a romantic evening with Riddhima.

Rohan took the CD that I had bought from a nearby Pune railway station and kept it on the dashboard of the car. He had worn a crisp white shirt and a pair of blue jeans to go with his Woodland shoes. He reached Riddhima's apartment and called her to come down. He was waiting outside the car, leaning on the door, and kept messaging her to come down soon.

Riddhima was fond of wearing makeup and junk jewellery, and was taking her own time to get ready, increasing Rohan's frustration in the process. She was wearing a magenta-coloured designer suit with zari work on it. She had teamed the outfit with silver jhumkis and jootis. She had gone light on the make-up this time, applying lots of kajal instead, which was Rohan's favourite. As she came outside the apartment, he was bowled over by how pretty she looked. 'How did I get so lucky?' he asked her as he hugged her tightly.

Rohan opened the door of the car for her like a perfect gentleman. 'What's that scent?' Riddhima asked as she took her seat. Rohan had kept a Milano Sandalwood car freshener in the car so the car smelled nice. Riddhima's face glowed in excitement as she inhaled the fragrance. She immediately planted a kiss on Rohan's cheek and held him by his arm as he drove the car.

After a few minutes, he told Riddhima to give him the CD that was kept over the dashboard. She saw the cover of the CD which '100 Romantic Hit Songs' written over it. Most of the songs were her favourite.

'Did you purchase it today?' she asked.

'Yes. I got the CD especially for you since you love these songs. After a lot of effort, I managed to find a CD with all your favourite numbers,' Rohan replied.

Riddhima's happiness was visible in her eyes. She inserted the CD into the player and was looking at the back cover of the CD that had the tracks written on it in chronological order.

'No disc,' the error message displayed on the screen.

I will kill Aditya if this CD doesn't play, thought Rohan. Keeping his fingers crossed, he ejected the CD and, like most guys do, rubbed it on his jeans as if cleaning it. He prayed to God that the CD would work. He didn't want to feel embarrassed in front of Riddhima.

'It will work. There is some problem with my player. It happens, sometimes,' he said trying to save his ass.

Once again, he inserted the CD into the player. Rohan was biting his fingernails in anticipation and praying it would work this time, and it did! A song came on and Rohan heaved a sigh of relief. Riddhima rested her head on his shoulders and began humming the song.

The song continued for few seconds and then abruptly changed to a new song before the earlier one could get over. In fact, it wasn't even a song! It was like two people were moaning while making out. Riddhima looked at him in shock and disgust. Rohan hurriedly pressed on a button to go back to the previous song but a message appeared on the screen saying *'Not applicable'*.

Riddhima looked at Rohan in anger, much like how we feel during Candy Crush when only one candy is left to crush and we run out of moves!

'What is this Rohan? You listen to such stuff?' Riddhima screamed.

'No. I mean…I didn't buy it.'

'What the fuck. You said that you had got this especially for me. So this is the quality of CD you get for me?'

Rohan didn't know what to tell her. He had planned to make her listen to all her favourite numbers, and instead what was playing was the audio of a B-grade porn movie. In a panicking state, he increased the volume instead of decreasing it, creating utter chaos inside the car. Riddhima yelled like mad and Rohan just hoped that her voice mixed with the sounds of the CD didn't become entertainment for other people on the road. Thankfully, the restaurant was nearby and they reached just before Riddhima could murder him.

I swear to God, I will never ever buy a pirated CD from a station, especially when I have to play it for my girlfriend. But I will never, NEVER, ask that ass Aditya, he thought.

Somehow, he managed to keep calm and held Riddhima's hand as he took her to the 9th floor which had the rooftop restaurant. She was still a bit upset about what had happened in the car but forgave him ultimately since she loved the innocent face that Rohan faked in front of her. By the time they reached the spot, the smile on her face was back.

The ambience of the restaurant was mesmeric. There was dim lighting and candles had been lit everywhere. Soft music was playing in the background. There was even a small pool around which some tables were laid. Couples could dip their feet in the pool and talk while they waited for dinner. Rohan had a print out of the discount coupon and showed it to the manager. He read the print out and showed them to a table by the pool. Rohan held out the seat for Riddhima and asked the waiter to get them the menus. Once done ordering the meal, Riddhima took Rohan by the hand and pulled her to sit near the pool, with their feet dipped in the water. Rohan went closer to her and kissed her on the cheek, saying,

'I love you, Riddhima. Happy Valentine's Day in advance. You are mine and will always be.'

Riddhima kissed him back and pulled his cheeks lovingly. It was like a dream come true for her, sitting beside her prince charming by the poolside,with candles around them and a perfect view of the city.

'Here is your wine, sir,' the waiter said handing them two glasses of wine.

They had ordered white wine with some Pasta, as offered in the deal.

'Cheers,' Rohan said as they clinked their glasses together.

No matter how many fights you get into or how many times you get upset, if you truly love a person, then even one look of theirs will bring a smile on your face.

'I want to spend all my future Valentine's Days with you. Promise me, even if we get busy, we will take out time from our schedules to celebrate our togetherness,' Riddhima stated.

'Yes. I am really lucky to have you in my life,' Rohan said kissing her hand.

Maybe the almighty had it all planned. Maybe he wanted Rohan to meet the wrong person before he could introduce her to the right person, so that he would know how to value her love. They both decided to confess their love to their parents to get their approval.

After spending a wonderful evening together, they decided to leave. Since the bill had already been paid through the online deal, they started to leave. But it really turned out to be their unlucky day because the manager came in with the pending bill, despite the online payment having been cleared. Rohan was shocked to see the bill.

'Sir, you had taken a deal which included 2 glasses of wine with which you got 2 complimentary ones as well. Plus, you were even served Pasta with it. But the deal didn't include the other dishes you ordered in the main course, sir. The pending bill is for that,' the manager explained.

'You should have told us beforehand what was included in the deal and what wasn't. How were we supposed to know?' Riddhima asked in annoyance.

'I am sorry, baby, for putting you through this.'

They had no option but to pay the pending amount. Sometimes if your luck changes for the better, it only lasts for so much before it changes again. Rohan's luck was certainly not on his side that day. The bad luck trickled down on me too as I got a couple of nasty messages from him saying *Bhenchod, teri maa ki aankh, saala gaandu*.

Not only did they have to pay the pending amount but, since Rohan had forgotten to carry his debit card, it was Riddhima who had to pay the pending amount for it.

Though, in my defense, I had told him to confirm whatever is included in the deal with the manager before he ordered anything. But he didn't. But his response to me was completely different from that of Riddhima. When a girlfriend says don't drink and drive, a guy's reply is *'You're so caring baby'* and when the same thing is said by a friend or a brother the reply is *'Apne baap ko mat sikha saale.'*

Though everything had not gone according to the plan, Riddhima was enjoying her time with Rohan and had no complaints at all. Rohan had parked the car in a secluded area after leaving the restaurant. His phone beeped with a message from Virat but he ignored the message as he wanted to end the date on a perfect note without any glitch. Virat had even messaged him while they were having dinner. He wanted to talk to Rohan about Mahek and so he wanted to ask him to meet. Rohan, however, ignored the message. It was a deserted road and there was no one around. Rohan took this opportunity to kiss Riddhima on the lips. His kiss came as a complete surprise to her, but a pleasant one. She returned his kiss with equal intensity. In that kiss, they felt like they had become one—in body and in soul.

There Can Never Be Another You

11th February, 2010
Virat's Apartment

'Virat, please think it over. If he tells his dad everything, it will create unnecessary complications in our relationship,' Mahek said trying to convince Virat.

Mahek had come to Virat's apartment in the evening to convince him not to go ahead with his plan, but he was adamant about confessing their relationship to Rohan and had even called him up but Rohan didn't take his call or reply to the message that he had sent him. Mahek was scared since she knew her family was quite conservative and did not support love affairs.

'You trust me?' Virat asked.

'Yes. More than myself,' Mehak replied with a sad face.

'Then leave everything to me. Why do you look so

terrified? Everything will be fine,' Virat smiled.

'Virat, you don't know my parents. They are kind of strict. That is the only reason I have never uploaded our pictures together on Orkut, forget about Facebook.'

'I understand your concern and I am taking full responsibility for it, Mahek. I love you more than I have ever loved anyone before and I am not taking such a step without giving a thought.'

For the past few days, Virat had been constantly thinking about whether he should tell Rohan everything. According to him, it was the right time to talk to him about Mahek as he had played a vital role in bringing back happiness to Rohan's life. He was confident that Rohan would take the news well and show support. He also knew that Rohan was not very frank with his parents and would not rat about their relationship to them. And if anything went wrong in the process, Mahek would be there to support him. The extent to which they trusted each other was extraordinary. They talked like best friends, fought like kids, argued like a married couple, and protected each other like siblings. Every girl wants a bad guy who will be good to her and every guy wants a good girl who will be bad to him. Virat may have dated many girls in the past but he treated Mahek like no other girl and she too gave the relationship her all, showering all her attention on him. They decided it was time to change the gear of their relationship and obtain a clearance certificate from Rohan.

'Are you sure?'

'Yes. We will celebrate Valentine's Day with him and Riddhima. Now give me a smile,' Virat said kissing her cheeks.

He called Rohan once again but this time too, he didn't respond. Finally, Virat decided to e-mail Rohan about it. By doing so, even Mahek would not have to face him directly. Mahek readily agreed after which Virat logged on to his Gmail account. Before mailing him, they thought of talking once to Kavya and take her opinion on it too. Though Virat had already discussed the entire matter with her, he still wanted to talk to her once to get her opinion on it. Her support and presence were of utmost importance to him.

'Kavya, we have finally decided to tell Rohan about our relationship. Do you think we are doing the right thing?' Virat asked as she answered the call.

'Please tell him that he is completely wrong,' Mahek screamed into the phone from behind Virat.

Kavya responded, 'If I had felt like you were doing something wrong, I would have stopped you yesterday itself. I will never let you do anything wrong until the day I am alive. Go ahead, my boy.'

'Kavya, at least you be on my side,' Mahek screamed into the phone again. Virat turned on the loudspeaker so that both could hear each other and he wouldn't go deaf in the process.

'If Virat wouldn't have taken this decision himself, I

would have forced him to. Hiding your relationship from Rohan is like almost breaking his trust, something his past girlfriend also did,' Kavya reminded them.

'Virat told you about Zoya too?' Mahek asked, snatching the phone from Virat.

'Yes. Don't worry. Everything will be fine.'

Kavya disconnected the call after wishing both of them luck, and also prayed for their togetherness. She wanted to be with them but the doctors had told her to rest for a few days. Virat and Mahek missed having her around but knew it was important for her to rest in order to recover faster.

It doesn't matter how strong your bonding with your friend is, even the strongest friendships are put to the test by love. The only man who could be as protective as her dad was her brother. Though Mahek was his cousin and they were never very frank with each other, he was his elder brother and nothing could change that. Virat was a bit nervous too but he was firm on his decision and Kavya's affirmative response made him stronger. Virat gave Kavya a peck on the cheek and told her not to worry too much. He then began typing the email.

Hey Rohan,

I know you will be confused looking at my mail. I tried to reach you through the phone but your number was either busy or not available. So I thought of mailing you since even Mahek was a bit afraid to talk directly to you. Eighty percent of relationships wouldn't have even begun if messaging service didn't exist. It has made our life so much easier. Oh yeah, you might be thinking how I know Mahek. Bro…no sorry…I can't call you bro now. You know that I'm a reticent person by nature, especially when it comes to my private life. That's the reason why I never shared any details with you about who I was seeing though you shared everything with me. Remember, I had told you that I was in love. The woman I'm in love with is none other than Mahek, your cousin. Trust me, I did not know she is your sister and neither did she know that we were friends and talked sometimes. It was only until a few days back when she saw you talking to me during your stay at her house that she came to know. She was afraid of facing you since she didn't know how you would react. But I didn't want to hide anything from you since we are friends and owe it to each other to tell the truth. The moment she told me everything, I decided to confess to you that I love her and am extremely serious about her. I know it comes as a big shock to you and you might even be angry at me but I promise you, if you have any issues with me, I will go away from Mahek's life forever. I will not even ask you a single question. But Rohan, I really love her and want to be with her forever. If you give us your support then Mahek and I would love to celebrate this Valentine's Day with Riddhima and you.

Love,

Virat

Virat re-read the entire mail once before clicking on the press button. After checking his outbox to see if the mail had in fact gone, he logged off. Mahek gave Virat a tight hug in appreciation of all the efforts he had been putting and the respect he had shown towards her brother Rohan. Every girl expects three things from her boyfriend—loyalty towards her, respect for her own space, and respect for her family. Virat had given her all three and more. So many times Virat had thought that he would never find someone to love him the way he needed to be loved. But Mahek had come into his life and showed him what true love really is.

Rohan and Riddhima's date ended with a long passionate kiss in the car. They spent some time together alone in the car, not only romancing but also laughing about the fun things they had done on their date. After dropping Riddhima on the way, he reached home and logged on to Gmail like he always did. Today, strangely, the first unread mail was from Virat.

Rohan read the mail for the fifth time that day. It wasn't what he was expecting. He had no clue about how he was supposed to react. Different thoughts were running through his mind and though he was not so close to Mahek and didn't share a great rapport with her, still she was his sister. He couldn't believe that Virat was dating her. The more he thought about it, the more the picture became clearer in his mind. He suddenly remembered that he had met Virat near Mahek's house in Aundh. He had even mentioned once that his girlfriend went to the same college. He felt like going to Virat's place and hitting him hard and abusing him, but he knew that was not going to help anyway. Moreover, Mahek would have lost all her faith in him. He kept calm and thought for some time. Then he called the both of them to fully understand what was happening.

Virat was confident about speaking with Rohan but Mehak was completely horrified and ignored Rohan's first few calls until Virat told her to answer it.

'Will you both tell me since when has this been going on?' Rohan asked.

'Rohan, we've been seeing each since mid-August but you have to believe me, I came to know about your relation with Mehak just a few days back when your family and you were at Mahek's home. I understand your concern but believe me, I am not with her just for fun. I am serious about her and want to marry her once I get to a place in my life where I can look after the both of us,' Virat said in a convincing tone.

'Bhaiya, I did not want to tell you this as I was afraid you might tell my parents. You know them well and I don't need to tell you how they would have reacted. Virat is not lying. In fact, he's the one who forced me to tell you this and not hide anything from you. Please Bhaiya, I am sorry for hiding the truth from you but I had no other option,' Mahek added in a low voice, afraid of facing Rohan's wrath.

'Is it true love or just infatuation? Virat, I had told you about my past relationship with Zoya and how it ended abruptly. I realized what true love is when I meet Riddhima. No doubt, I loved Zoya but Riddhima gave me a feeling of what true love is and taught me how to love back. Mehak, you also know about Zoya. Don't you?'

'Rohan, I only want to say that I will make your sister really happy. I won't say those filmy dialogues that I will never bring tears to her eyes and so on, because we go through so much in our lives that tears are bound to fall. But whenever they will fall from her eyes, I will be there to catch them.'

'Bhaiya, I really love Virat and my life will be a living hell without him. Please. I am sorry. I will always share everything with you. It's a promise from a sister to her brother,' Mahek added.

After a brief conversation, Rohan hung up the phone without giving his verdict on their relationship. Virat and Mahek became nervous as Rohan had said nothing about whether he had accepted their relationship or not. Mahek cried thinking Rohan would tell everything to her parents and their lives would become a complete mess. Virat continuously tried to calm her down but somewhere even he was worried about their relationship, now that he had got no response from Rohan. Rohan on the other side didn't wanted to express what he felt about the entire episode. He was worried about Mahek and it was obvious that, being a brother, he would be protective of her. But somewhere, he had blind trust on Virat and knew that he won't fool around with Mahek. The way he had helped him move on with his life made it evident that he valued relationships and believed in making others happy. After thinking for a few hours, he sent the same message to both of them:

Just because I am okay with your relationship doesn't mean you cross all your limits. And one thing you both have to promise me is that you won't divert your mind from studies till your college gets over and also from each other till life gets over.

Virat screamed in happiness when he read the message. He immediately messaged Rohan,

I won't make the second promise because I don't want to divert my mind from Mahek even after my life is over. My love for her is not limited to this lifetime. It's far beyond that. Thanks for supporting us. Also, I need to tell you one extremely important thing related to your life. Please don't ignore it or take it lightly. I feel that it you should know this since it's never easy to face the truth. I will tell you once we meet on 13th evening.

Mehak wrote to Rohan saying,

Love you, Bhaiya. You are the best brother in this whole world. Thanks for understanding my love and not reacting negatively like typical brothers. Now I can share everything with you. Earlier I used to think that you are bit khadus type. But I was wrong. Love you.

In our entire lives, we get one chance to build a relationship with someone and to win that person's trust. If you lose that trust, then even though you may do all sort of things to please him, you can never share the same bonding with him again. By accepting Virat and Mahek's relationship, Rohan had not only showed faith in friendship but had also gained Mahek's love forever. Rohan had decided that everyone would celebrate Valentine's Day together at Riddhima's apartment by gathering on the eve of 13th February and celebrating till the stroke of midnight. This 14th February was indeed special as all the relationships were inching towards a perfect end. Virat and Mahek were excited to be together for the first time in the presence of Rohan and had also informed Kavya about how well he had received them. Kavya was also going to join them for the Valentine's bash.

Riddhima and Rohan had both gone through a lot in their lives before entering into a relationship with each other, but now they were truly, madly, and deeply in love.

Virat had unknowingly helped in breaking the walls of awkwardness between Rohan and Mahek. There's no other love like the love *for* a brother and there's no other love like the love *of* a brother. It's amazing how we can touch each other's lives without even realizing it.

13th February, 2010
German Bakery, Koregaon Park

'Mehak is going to pick you up from your place. I will come a bit later as I have a few surprises planned for everyone,' Virat told Kavya over the phone.

Virat wanted to take gifts for everyone and had thus told Mahek to pick up Kavya from her home and reach Riddhima's apartment. He was on cloud nine and it called for a double celebration because not only was it their first Valentine's together, even Rohan had accepted their relationship. He was slightly tensed about unfolding that one secret to Rohan that Mahek had disclosed to him, but he wanted to start the new phase of their relationship on a clean state and didn't want to hide anything from anyone. Anyway, it was party time and he had planned to unfold the secret without spoiling anyone's mood. After buying all the gifts from the shopping mall at Koregaon Park, he went to German Bakery to eat something since he was starving and hadn't eaten all day. While at the bakery, he thought of buying red velvet cake for Rohan since he remembered

Rohan mentioning to him it was his favourite.

'Are you going to German Bakery?' Kavya asked him. 'Please, bring some sandwiches for me. I love them.'

'You know what, I do more work for you than I do for my girlfriend,' Virat smiled.

'Shut up. Don't tell me what I already know. I know how much you care for her.'

'But I love you more. If you would have not introduced me to her, I would have never realized the meaning of true love,' Virat said as he searched for a table in the bakery.

'Don't get sentimental now. Bye. And don't forget the sandwiches.'

Kavya hung up the phone quickly as Mahek had already reached. Virat ordered sandwiches for Kavya, the red velvet cake for Rohan, and a burger for him to eat. He thought of all that they had gone through these past few days and how everything was now finally coming into place. It made him think about how life is so unpredictable because when he first started chatting with Rohan, he could never imaginehe would feel so connected to him. He was content with his life because he had a friend like Kavya, a girlfriend like Mahek, and Rohan as his brother-in-law.

Finishing off the burger, he messaged Mehak in delight,

Everytime I see you, I feel a little flame in my heart that lights up because I love you. If I am given a chance to love again, I would still choose you because you're the password to my life. Happy Valentine's Day. The celebrations will begin in some time.

Virat looked at the message and smiled again. His happiness reflected in his eyes. He looked around to check if his parcel was ready. The waiter told him it would take some more time since the place was packed with customers. It was 7 pm and many of the foreigners at the bakery had left for the Osho Ashram for their daily meditation session. Since his wait had been prolonged, he was scrolling through his picture folder and looking and pictures of him with Mahek and Kavya—the two people who had brought so much joy into his life. Just then, he received a call from Rohan.

'What time will you be reaching?'

'I am on my way. Just waiting to collect the order. I will be there around 7.45 pm,' Virat said, looking at his watch.

'Hurry up! I can't wait to see you, particularly for two reasons: Firstly, I want to see you as my sister's boyfriend and secondly, I want to hear the important thing that you were talking about,' Rohan said.

'Even I am keen to meet you for two reasons: Firstly, to see you as my girlfriend's brother and secondly, to meet the two people dearest to you in life: Riddhima and Aditya,' Virat added.

'They both are with me. Come soon.'

'I have more surprises for all of you and let's make this evening…'

Before he could complete the sentence, there was a huge blast in the bakery.

People began running helter-skelter in the café. The massive explosion that had taken everybody by surprise. The sound was absolutely deafening and all the windows of the bakery had been shattered. Everyone started screaming in terror when they saw a couple of bodies lying on the ground in a pool of blood. There was a lot of smoke and dust and people started panicking.

Everything went black in front of Virat's eyesas he lay on floor, sandwiched between a hot metal and a pillar with his arm completely dislocated from his body. The weight of the metal pressed against his upper body, making him cry out in pain. He couldn't move even an inch and with smoke all around, he couldn't breathe. All he could feel was the metal stamping on his body. He lied there, motionless, counting his last breaths. There were dead and injured people lying in a pool of blood everywhere. Some other people on the floor were crying out in pain. People had died, lost their arms, their limbs, and their heads. The smoke from the explosion escaped the bakery and clouded the street outside.

Virat didn't want to die like this; without even saying a last goodbye to Mahek, the girl he wanted to marry, be a caring husband to, and with whom he wanted to father a child. He wanted to live for Kavya as he was her life. Her best friend and her moral support. How could life end like this? Just when everything around him had started regaining normalcy, this had to happen. Virat cursed his fate for having played such a cruel joke on him. Before closing his eyes, he prayed that no one would recognize him as he knew that Mahek and Kavya would suffer a mental breakdown if they came to know that he was dying! The gifts that were wrapped with yellow paper had turned red with his blood, and Virat lay there waiting for death to hit him and shut the curtains of his life forever.

Death is so uncertain. One moment you're sitting with the person dearest to you and the very next moment, you lose him forever. It's said no one stays with you forever but when you lose someone midway, how can you fill the void that the person's absence creates? Time can heal but never erase past wounds. All the dreams that Virat had seen with Mahek and Kavya remained unfulfilled. Virat breathed his last that day.

Dreams Are For Real

'His phone's unreachable. The last I spoke with him, he told me he'd be reaching in half an hour,' Rohan said looking at the time on his wristwatch.

'Maybe there's some network issue. Let's wait for him,' I said as I placed the cake and a bottle of champagne on the table.

Everyone had assembled by then and were waiting for Virat to come so that the celebrations could begin. Except for Rohan, I was meeting everyone for the first time. I found Riddhima extremely cute. The love she had for Rohan was visible in her eyes. One could tell Kavya was a real fighter and Virat and Mahek were her backbone with the way she spoke about them so lovingly. She was extremely lively and her indomitable spirit impressed me a lot. Though Mahek was Rohan's cousin, we had never met each other before. She came across as really sweet too and we got along well. Starters and cold drinks had been served and everyone seemed to be having a good time.

Mehak was sipping on her drink and casually scrolling through the website of a newspaper when one particular headline caught her eye: *Severe Bomb Blast at German Bakery; a few casualties reported*

She almost fell down in shock and caught hold of a nearby railing for support. *Virat is at the German Bakery*!! she thought. Immediately, she dialled his number but couldn't get through to him. She began to panic. She showed us the message and I quickly switched on the TV to see the live coverage. Everyone was on the verge of tears, praying from him to be safe. We were completely shocked and didn't know what to do. We had seen a lot of news reports on blasts in the country before and had never bothered about it before, but this time we had someone close to us on the spot of the blast. We didn't dare to think what could have happened to him. Mehak and Kavya who were sobbing continuously. They tried every possible way to get in touch with Virat but couldn't.

On one of the news channels, the reporter was saying:

Latest report coming in from the site of the blast. At least 6 people have been reported dead and more than 30 injured after a massive bomb blast hit the German Bakery. Why did the terrorists pick German Bakery as their venue? Lots of unanswered questions...

We immediately switched off the TV and left for the bakery with the hope that Virat would be safe. Words cannot describe such situations.

With heavy steps, we made our way to the car, constantly praying for everything to be okay. Rohan was driving the car at an extremely fast pace, skipping all the traffic signals so we could reach as soon as possible. But most of the roads leading to German Bakery had been shut by the police. There was nakabandi all around. We asked a few police officers where the victims' bodies had been taken and they gave us the name of a hospital. We decided to head straight to the hospital instead of the bakery. Mahek and I kept trying to call Virat on his mobile number in the hope that he might pick up and say, 'Dude, I'm fine. Where's the beer?' Though none of use wanted to acknowledge it, by now we were almost certain that something dreadful had happened to him.

The entrance to the hospital was jam-packed. Lots of injured people were being wheeled inside. Some had an arm missing, some a leg. It looked like a war had broken out in the city. Media and relatives had gathered around the place, and all we could hear were the cries of people who had lost their closed ones. There were parents sobbing because they had lost their only child; there were brothers crying since their sisters had been injured; there were wives crying since they had lost their husband forever. It was a painful sight to watch and I decided to wait with Kavya outside since she was howling uncontrollably.

When we got to the mortuary, there were many bodies lying on the ground covered with white sheets. Rohan, Mahek, and Riddhima went inside to verify if Virat was one of the casualties of the incident. Kavya and I waited outside in nervous anticipation. With trembling hands, Rohan removed the white sheet from one of the victims' bodies. When he saw the face, our worst fears came true—it was Virat! Mahek broke down completely and started screaming. She tried to go close to him, but the doctors stopped her. Her weeping reached Kavya's ears and she gripped my arm tightly. When Rohan came out and told us that Virat was no more, Kavya fell down on the floor. Rohan and Riddhima tried to console Mahek while I picked up Kavya and helped her to a nearby bench, giving her some water to drink.

'How could he leave me like this? He was my stick to walk; I saw the world through his eyes,' Kavya cried.

We have no control over fate. We have to accept the fact that people who are close to us will die, sooner or later. But when someone leaves you unexpectedly, it hurts even more. When a person who is in the prime of his life leaves so suddenly, with any warning or explanations, it takes you by complete surprise. We felt like our world had been turned upside down.

Virat was the beat of Mehak's heart, the soul of her body, the reason for his existence. Her life had come to a standstill after his death. It was hard for Mehak to stop thinking about him and burn to ashes all hopes of their future, when they might still have lived and loved together, and raised their kids together. He was the person Kavya knew she could turn to when she needed help. He was her moral support, someone to chill with. She cursed God for not having taken away her life instead. She survived an accident in the past, but lost the meaning of her life with Virat's departure.

Virat had shown Rohan how to live and be truly happy and had given him the inspiration to live with the one who truly loved him. But when it was time to return the same love, Virat had left him. I had met him only once and had found him to be extremely friendly and full of life. Riddhima and I couldn't control our emotions and let our tears flow. We did the paperwork to get his body released from the hospital. It's strange how a person ceases to exist after his death and how we refer to him as just a 'body'. Rohan and I made all the necessary arrangements for the last rites. Finally, we bid adieu to Virat forever in front of his family and close friends.

Even though Virat was gone forever, his memory would always livewith us, comforting us in our darkest nights. Virat would be missed every minute of every day.

16th February, 2010
Rohan's residence

'Rohan, I have to leave. I've been in Pune for a really long time, and I think it's time for me to return to Mumbai now,' I said while we had our breakfast together.

It had been a week sinceVirat's death. I had extended my stay and had to return to Mumbai even if I didn't want to. Rohan remained silent, lost in his thoughts. Virat's loss had really affected him badly. I told him he had to overcome his grief for Virat's sake saying he wouldn't have liked to see him in such a condition. I made him understand that after Virat's death, he was responsible for two other lives—Kavya, who had lost her only best friend and Mahek, who had lost the love of her life.

'You have to take care of both the girls. It's not an easy for them to overcome the loss and you as Rohan's friend have to try to keep them as happy as possible. Especially Kavya, because Virat was her backbone. Also, you need to make Mahek strong enough to cope up with life. Her support will be vital for Kavya's recovery too,' I explained. Moving on was the only way he could go.

'I know that I am the one who has to take care of everyone but it's not going to be easy for me,' Rohan stated.

'I agree, but if you fall weak, what will happen to the others? They will be completely shattered. You have to be strong and spread happiness all around. Regardless of what problems Virat had in his life, he always helped others and was there for you too. It's your time to fill his void and be there for Mahek and Kavya. I am sure Riddhima feels the same way as I do about this.'

Rohan nodded and hugged me before I could leave.

'By the way, I didn't get a chance to tell you that day, but I really like my bhabi. Riddhima is the perfect girl to handle an ass like you. Never leave her or hurt her. Or else I will kill you,' I said to lighten the mood.

'Thanks Aditya, not just for all your support but also for staying here with us, even when you had to go to college in Mumbai,' Rohan said in a deep voice.

I left. I lived. I learned. Virat was so full of positivity that some of it had rubbed off on me too. He taught me that life cannot be lived according to your plans, and you have to be prepared for the unexpected. Everything happens for a reason; however hard it may be. It's just sometimes hard to find those reasons. Sometimes you have to sacrifice your dreams just to be with the one you love. Living your life with them is much better than living your dream alone. Virat had left, forever, but he had left behind memories that would always bring a smile on everyone's face. When I came to Pune, I never thought that I would be acquainted with the lives of so many people who would teach me a new way of living. Mahek had taught me what love was, Kavya had introduced me to the real meaning of friendship, Riddhima had made me realize that waiting for a loved one was worth it, and Virat had shed light upon what life was and had taken me closer to my ownself. Indeed, people like him don't come often into our lives. Even after reaching Mumbai, I kept thinking about them and how the experience had enriched me and made me a better person.

Even after a fortnight, everytime the phone rang, Mahek would pick up hoping it was Virat. It was impossible for them to believe that they would never see him again. Many a times, Mahek would take her anger out on Rohan, but Rohan was playing the role of the perfect elder brother by keeping his calm and by trying to make her smile. The sudden demise of Virat had made Rohan and Mahek connect with each other at an emotional level.

With the passage of time, they slowly started accepting what had happened, though it was not a happy acceptance. Kavya too was trying to regain her energy and hope by accepting the bitter truth; though at times she would feel listless and lifeless, discouraged, and sometimes, depressed. It was the winter of their grief – a long, slow, dormant period. But Mahek knew she had to be tough because Kavya needed her as a friend. Everyone was supporting each other and Virat had played the role of a catalyst by bringing them together.

The whole process of recovering from the grief of having lost a loved one had changed them as individuals. They were not the same people they had been before. They had grown from that experience and it was evident by their changed outlook towards relationships and life in general.

We always ignore people who are close to us—friends, parents, girlfriends, boyfriends—and forget to appreciate their presence in our lives. What if you lose them suddenly, forever? Even the thought of it makes us shiver. Rohan, Mahek, and Kavya, along with Riddhima, had forged a new relationship with each other; of togetherness and friendship. By slowly accepting their grief, they had taken the path towards healing. Losing Virat so unexpectedly was hard for all of us; but he had left behind an indelible footprint in our hearts and memories to keep us going.

Everything Happens For a Reason

28th February, 2010

It was Sunday morning and Rohan had met Mehak for a morning walk at a nearby park. He wanted to spend some time with her and see how she was doing. The early sunrise brought with it a new ray of hope in their lives and gave them the strength they needed to overcome their past and move on. They had become good friends since that incident and were now emotionally connected to each other.

'Everytime I would see my friends having fun with their brothers, I would get upset as I am a single child and don't even have a close cousin whom I can talk to. Their brothers would pick them up after college and take them out for coffee. I always wanted a brother whom I could talk to, take guidance from, and share my feelings with. Around the time of my marriage, he would cry for me and give me strength to be a part of a new family. Thank you, Bhaiya. I am so proud to have you in my life,' Mahek said walking along with Rohan on the jogging track.

After the walk, they went and sat on a nearby bench. He wiped the tears from her eyes and pulled her cheeks, trying to make her smile.

'I don't know what to say. I have a sister with whom I can share my life now but at the cost of losing my friend. And I don't know whether to thank that friend for breaking the barriers between us unknowingly or apologize to him that I couldn't give your hand to him. It was not easy for me but Aditya's words always made me strong and though I know that no one can take Virat's place, I am trying to make you smile and get over the past.'

'Bhaiya, please don't be sorry. I am sure if Virat was alive today he would have felt proud of you. I wish I could have shared everything with you from the beginning, looking at the way you have handled Kavya and me these past few days, helping us get back to normal.'

'I just want you all to smile again for Virat. He always wanted everyone to be together and we should not disappoint him.'

'I know I can never take Virat's place but after him, I am the only one to look after Kavya. So even if I feel like breaking down, I can't. One question that keeps echoing in my head is that, "Is the value of our lives so little?" If I wouldn't have told him to bring all those gifts, he wouldn't have gone to that area.'

She leaned on Rohan's shoulder and he patted her head gently. Rohan had entered her life at a time when she desperately needed a friend. She was lucky to have found a friend and brother in Rohan. After taking a couple of rounds in the park, they lay down on the grass, talking about Riddhima and how Rohan had proposed to her. She too shared all the crazy moments she had spent with Virat and Kavya and how they would annoy people around them with their acts. Mahek was supposed to meet Kavya directly at the park, and Rohan decided to join them since Riddhima was busy with her Sunday classes and he had nothing better to do.

Rohan and Mahek were connected emotionally in Virat's absence and even he might be looking down from the skies, content with the change his absence had brought in their lives.

De-Katta, Kothrud

'How strange it is that we all are sitting here, but the person who introduced us is missing,' Kavya said opening a packet of chips.

'Yes, but we will always be with you and you can treat

me as your elder brother or as your friend, whatever you feel like. I promise, you will never feel alone. Virat was my friend too, and so, according to the law, we are close friends too,' Rohan smiled.

Good relationships don't just happen overnight. They take time and patience to nurture. All three of them had gone through hard times and valued the presence of each other in their lives. They met whenever they found the time to, and though they didn't interact much, whenever they did, they had a great time with each other. Maybe, the best kind of friends are who you can sit with on a porch and then walk away feeling like it was the best conversation you ever had. They shared a somewhat similar relationship. Mahek always missed Virat and remembered their college days together. She knew that Virat had more affection towards Kavya than her as their friendship was immortal. But she didn't mind it one bit since Kavya was an equally good friend to her. They were having their Sunday brunch together and catching up on old times.

'I still have the last message he sent me almost few minutes before…' Mehak paused.

She was going through her inbox and read the message aloud.

If I am given a chance to love again, I would still choose you as you're the password to my life. Happy Valentine's Day. The celebrations will begin in some time.

'But before the celebration could actually begin, he left,' Kavya said in a deep voice and continued, 'If I would not have told him to bring sandwiches for me, he would have left the place a few minutes before the blast and would have been sitting with us today.'

'Guys, do not take the blame on you. We cannot change things. We need to move on because even Virat won't be happy to see us cry like this,' Rohan said trying to change the topic.

Rohan was missing him too. There are moments in life when you miss someone so much that you just want them to appear in front of you and hug them for real. He hid his pain with a smile on his face. To avoid making eye contact, he kept browsing his phone and opened his inbox to see Virat's message.

Also, I need to tell you one extremely important thing related to your life. Please don't ignore it or take it lightly. I feel that you should know this since it's never easy to face the truth. I will tell you once we meet on 13th evening.

Suddenly, he remembered that Virat had wanted to tell him something crucial about his life that day. Rohan was curious and asked Mehak if Virat had mentioned anything about it to her. She knew exactly what Rohan was talking about, becauseVirat had discussed it with her before revealing the truth to Rohan. She had kept it a secret from him since the past few months. But, as the equation had changed between them, she decided to tell him the truth. The truth that would give him the shock of his life.

9th February, 2010
Virat's residence

'There is one more thing that I want to tell you. I have never shared this with anyone before, but I feel like telling you,' Mahek said.

Virat was barely trying to digest the shock of accepting the fact that Mahek was Rohan's sister when Mahek was unfolding another secret.

'Now what? Have you decided to give me an attack tonight? I don't want to die so soon,' Virat winked.

However, when he heard the secret, he couldn't believe his ears.

'Rohan's previous girlfriend Zoya had lied to him that she couldn't take their relationship ahead because her family would be against it,' Mahek disclosed.

'I remember Rohan telling me the same thing when we discussed it.'

'Actually, the truth is that…'

'What is it? Tell me,' Virat shouted.

'Zoya had been tested positive for HIVwhich is why she

was leaving the city forever with her family. She wanted Rohan to live his life happily without any complications and had hence kept the truth hidden from him. She wanted him to live with someone who truly loved him so that she could die content knowing that someone is taking care of him. Her family was taking her to Shimla for treatment but she knew the outcome. We were in touch occasionally and she had told me about this before she left. I had promised her that I will not to tell Rohan, ever, about this.'

Virat couldn't even imagine something so terrible. He didn't even move from his seat and had tears in his eyes. T*his was not something that should be kept hidden from Rohan,* he thought. He somehow convinced Mehak that they should tell Rohan about their relationship and about Zoya too, on the 13th evening. Though Mahek didn't want to and was extremely frightened, Virat had made up his mind and even Kavya had given him the green signal.

28th February, 2010
De-Katta, Kothrud

'Bhaiya, Virat wanted to tell you this that evening but...' Mahek cried.

Rohan was stunned by what she had just told her. Though she was his past now and he had moved on with his life, he felt the situation could have been handled in a better fashion had she mentioned it once to him. We are so quick in judging another person that we hardly think there could be another reason for the decisions they take. Rohan never thought that this could be the reason why Zoya would separate from him. He shut his eyes and prayed for forgiveness for having taken her wrongly.

I am already tense so please don't make me weaker. You are my strength and you should always smile. I even talked to your sister about it and she too agrees with me. Rohan, please understand that we just can't be together. Remember, someone somewhere is happy knowing that you are happy. So always smile and work hard achieve your dreams.

He recollected everything she had told him. But he was still angry at Zoya for not having told him the truth. How could she face such a trauma all alone? She always wanted him to grow in life and love someone who loved him more than her.

Her words echoed in his ears:

Listen, look for a girlfriend who loves you, and don't go for just looks. She should be able to take care of you in hard times and understand your needs. Got it? Promise me that you will inform me when you will find her.

Mehak got up from her seat and sat beside Rohan holding his hand, comforting him.

'Virat had even planned to book your tickets to Shimla so that you could meet her once.'

'That means you know where she is in Shimla?' Rohan stammered.

'Yes.'

'Rohan you should meet Zoya once,' Kavya added.

'Even you knew about it?'

'Yes. Virat had told me that he was going to tell you all about it that evening. I was proud that he had taken the right decision and supported him. You should be happy that you had a friend like him,' Kavya smiled.

Rohan stared at her, and then turned towards Mahek. She smiled and nodded her head in support. It was Virat's wish too ,which sadly turned out to be one of his last wishes. Both Kavya and Mahek tried to cheer him up and asked him to go to meet Zoya once. Rohan was confused whether Riddhima would agree to it or not. Kavya made him understand that Riddhima loved him with a true heart and would gladly let him go.

Everything happens for a reason. Sometimes we can figure out the reason in time and sometimes not. He told everything to Riddhima that evening after her classes.

'I trust you' she said without hesitation. It was then that he realized that 'I trust you' made him feel better than 'I love you'. True love is not about those phone calls or kiss

emoticons that are sent through messages, but it is the silent smiles and knowing your other half better than yourself. Riddhima gave Rohan a tight warm hug for keeping faith in her and telling her about Zoya like he used to before their relationship.

One should never blame their love without knowing the whole reality behind their decision. Zoya had shown a different side of true love by opting to move out of Rohan's life and now it was his turn to fulfil the promise that Zoya had asked him to keep; to inform her when he finds someone who could take care of him in hard times and understand his needs. Rohan and Riddhima decided to go to Shimla to meet Zoya one last time.

2nd March, 2010
Pune Airport

'Just think what would've happened had Virat never come into our lives and enriched it the way he did?' Rohan asked Riddhimaas they sat in the waiting lounge.

'Maybe, life isn't about finding your other half. Maybe, it's about finding yourself. I am happy that he brought so many positive changes in you. Mehak lost the love of her life and I know it feels terrible, but today she is smiling because she found a wonderful a brother in you who is more than a friend to her. Kavya, too got a friend in you. I love you so much for being a real man,' Riddhima smiled.

It's not easy to handle one woman at a time and Rohan was handling three of them! He was playing the role of a friend, a brother and a lover, flawlessly. He was madly in love with Riddhima but had never made it his weakness. They waited at the airport to board their flight to Shimla and thought of how different life would've been had Virat not been a part of it. There is a reason why we meet every person in our lives. Some test you, some use you, some teach you a lesson, while some bring out the best or worst in you. Virat had transformed Rohan as a person completely, and had unlocked the password to his life. Wherever he is now, he'd be smiling looking down at them. Even Mehak and Kavya had understood that the past can never come back, even if we cling on to it too tightly. So it's best to let go. Moving on is never easy but sometimes it's necessary!

Epilogue

Almost half a decade has passed since Virat's death and Mehak has now started her own salsa training classes after completing her graduation. She is soon going to start her own event management company. At times she misses Virat's presence while teaching dance to her students but his absence doesn't let her down but encourages her to do well in life.

Kavya is still Mahek's BFF and they still do the same crazy things together. They have their share of arguments like all friends do. After all, friends are never true friends unless you've had arguments and then become friends again. Because of so many people around her who genuinely cared for her, her smile was back, as was her madness. She was now driving her bike around the city too. How you may ask? Because her vision was back. Yes, she had an eye operation that resurrected her eyesight and brought back the colours in her life. It was initially hard for her to get accustomed to the fact that Virat would no longer be in front of her. But the love from everyone made her stronger and allowed her to move on in life. She is now working for an NGO who looks for the betterment of orphaned children.

Rohan had found his forever in Riddhima and both are now happily married to each other. They are indeed the perfect couple who stand by each other through thick and thin. They even have a cute daughter who looks exactly like Rohan and is very naughty. She wants a smartphone like her dad even though she doesn't know how to operate it.

Some people often think moving on is impossible but that is because they never felt unconditional love. Riddhima not only loved Rohan, she also made him a better person. They still visit Zoya occassionally while she continues her battle against HIV. Zoya had accepted that Rohan and she were never meant to be, but they loved every single second that they had spent together. She still keeps the gift that Riddhima had given her when they met for the first time.

3rd March, 2010
Shimla

Everyone needs love. Some strive hard for it while others get it for free. Zoya had been striving for it for long. One of the hardest things in the world is keeping your mouth shut when you know something needs to be said. When she saw Rohan in front of her, it was like meeting someone you had lost years back and had no hope of them coming back. It was a huge surprise for her to see her love back after such a long time. They just stood in front of each other without knowing what to say. Zoya understood why Rohan had come to meet her as she had hardly told anyone about her stay in Shimla except for Mahek and a few others.

'How are you?' Rohan asked.

'What should I say? This is the most difficult question for me these days. I can't even say that I am fine.'

'You should have...at least...you know...told me once...' Rohan stammered.

'You would have never moved on had I told you, and even if you did, you would have never loved anyone like you, loved me,' Zoya said.

Noticing the girl standing behind Rohan, she asked, 'Who is she?'

'My girlfriend, Riddhima'

Though she knew about Riddhima, to actually see him with her was a bit tough for her to accept. Even though you may seem to have moved on with your life, if a fragment of your past confronts you, it takes you by complete surprise. However, Zoya was cordial and exchanged smiles with her. She did not want to put up a pretence since she was aware that Rohan can't be part of her life even if she wants him to. She wanted a better life for him and had made the decision to go away from his life herself. No matter how strong a girl can be, sometimes all she needs is a hug. There was a wave of awkwardness in the room.

'I am happy for you. So you kept your promise,' Zoya said breaking the silence.

Zoya looked at Riddhima who brought out a gift from her bag and handed it to her. It was an idol of Lord Ganesh. Zoya thanked her and Riddhima gave her a friendly hug in return. Rohan smiled looking at the gesture. He felt really lucky to have an understanding and big-hearted girl like Riddhima in his life. It takes courage for a girl to meet her boyfriend's ex-girlfriend as a well-wisher.

'Friends?' Riddhima said extending a hand of friendship towards Zoya.

Zoya was surprised and glanced at Rohan for a second. Rohan just smiled.

'We can at least be friends,' he added.

She smiled and offered her hand in return. She now had no regrets in life now and could rejoice in these moments till her last breath. After spending a few hours with her, they were about to leave,when Zoya asked,

'Oh crap, amidst the excitement I forgot to ask you about Virat. How is he?'

Rohan and Riddhima didn't know what to tell her. They were also surprised that she knew about Virat since none of them had talked about Virat with her. It was then she told them that Virat had called her when he came to know about her condition just to wish her well. He had promised Zoya that Rohan would meet her once for sure.

'Say my thanks to him as he fulfilled his promise too,' Zoya said as she bid a goodbye to them.

They smiled and left without telling her about his demise as they didn't want to snatch the smile from her face.

Is this the end? Nah! It's just the beginning of a lifetime of friendship. Don't let life pass you by, because any moment could be that moment that changes the rest of your life! Every person in my life has transformed me in some way or the other and I can't imagine what life would have been without them. Everytime I find myself in the middle of nowhere, I find my true self. Everytime I visit Pune, I meet all of them. Mehak has tried teaching me Salsa so many times but has failed miserably. Now even she has realized that I have two left feet.

Friendship is silent, unwritten, unbreakable by distance, unchangeable with time! Virat had changed their lives forever and each of them carried a piece of him in their hearts. He never defined friendship. He knew friendship meant different things to different people. He only knew of its unifying power and how it can bring people closer. He had shown everyone how friendship is the only 'ship' that doesn't sink.

Acknowledgements

Some moments change our lives forever. Many such moments since the release of my first book *Few Things Left Unsaid* in 2011 have made me the person I am today. I would like to thank my millions of readers all over the world for their unflinching love and support. You all mean the world to me!

All the people I thank below have been my strength while I finished writing the book.

To Dipika Tanna and Jasmine Sethi for reading the manuscript at Rajnikanth's pace as many times as I requested them.

To Mrunmayee Ambekar for their honest reviews and selfless support.

To Saurabh More just because I mentioned his name the last time and it worked for me.

To Priyanka Dhasade for criticizing me throughout the process and provoking me to write better.

To Neha Maheshwari and Mrunmayi Dhurandar for forcing their friends to read the draft, even if they were not interested.

To Apurva for guiding me all the time and Sonja D' Silva for tolerating my nonsensical talks.

To Kalyani Akolkar for being extremely patient in answering my numerous questions, Neha Karandikar for her constant opinions on my work, and Simran Vegad for her valuable inputs.

To Manik Jaiswal, Zankrut Oza and Narendra Singh for their open-handed promotions and Abhilash Ruhela for reviewing my books and making me realize that he's not an easy person to impress.

To all the people who really matter—mom, dad, and my sister Shweta, and my grandparents for their humble support. Love you all!

To God, for being kind to me when it comes to writing.

To my extended family on Facebook and Twitter.

To Milee Ashwarya, Gurveen Chadha, Shruti Katoch, and the entire team at Random House India for being kind enough even when I miss their deadlines.

Lastly, a big thank you to my growing family of readers.

Love you forever and hamesha!

A Note on the Author

Sudeep Nagarkar is a popular contemporary Indian writer and has authored four bestselling novels –*Few Things Left Unsaid* (2011), *That's the Way We Met* (2012), *It Started With a Friend Request* (2013), and *Sorry You're Not My Type* (2014).

All his books continue to top the bestseller charts since their release. He is the recipient of the 2013 Youth Achievers' Award.

After completing his Engineering from Mumbai, he pursued management studies from Welingkar Institute of Mangement and now also writes for television. He has given guest lectures in various renowned institutes and organizations.

For more information about Sudeep, you can visit www.sudeepnagarkar.in or get in touch with Sudeep via his:

Facebook fan page: facebook.com/sudeepnagarkar.official.fanpage

Facebook profile: facebook.com/sudeep.nagarkar

Twitter handle: sudeep_nagarkar

Email: contact@sudeepnagarkar.in